# WOLF HOLLOW

## Also available by Victoria Houston

### The Loon Lake Fishing Mysteries

# WOLF HOLLOW

## A Lew Ferris
## Mystery

# VICTORIA HOUSTON

CROOKED
LANE

NEW YORK

Published in the United States by Crooked Lane Books, an imprint of The Quick Brown Fox & Company LLC.

Crooked Lane Books and its logo are trademarks of The Quick Brown Fox & Company LLC.

Library of Congress Catalog-in-Publication data available upon request.

ISBN (hardcover): 978-1-64385-800-5
ISBN (ebook): 978-1-64385-801-2

Cover design by Nicole Lecht

Printed in the United States.

www.crookedlanebooks.com

Crooked Lane Books
34 West 27th St., 10th Floor
New York, NY 10001

First Edition: January 2022

10 9 8 7 6 5 4 3 2 1

*For Mike*

Tell me the landscape in which you live and I will tell you who you are.

> —Ortega y Gassett, Spanish philosopher

# Chapter One

❧

It was a sunny May afternoon in Loon Lake, Wisconsin, and middle-school kids from Curran School were crowding into Sweo's Gas & Groceries for after-school treats. Down in the DVD aisle three boys and a girl lurked, eyes on the entrance to the convenience store. The tallest of the seventh-graders checked his watch and whispered, "Three thirty, guys. Get ready. . . ."

Two minutes later the door opened and a man in his twenties, dressed in crisply ironed khaki slacks and a light-blue shirt, sleeves rolled up, walked in. After a quick glance around the buzzing shop, he headed straight for the DVD aisle. Spotting the dark-haired girl, he smiled and held out his phone, matching the Instagram photo he'd received the day before from the young girl looking at him. As he moved toward her, she raised her right hand. Two boys emerged from where they had been hiding at the end of the aisle. The third boy ran for the door.

"Stop, right there, Mister. This is a citizens' arrest," said the boy named Larry.

The man, confusion on his face, hesitated, then turned and ran out the door. Jumping into his car, he didn't notice the boy standing behind the black Range Rover, his phone at the ready to shoot a photo of the car's license plate.

\* \* \*

Over in the Loon Lake police department, Chief Lewellyn Ferris studied the bumper sticker that had been laid across her desk. In bright-blue letters against a white background outlined in red it read *Lew for Sheriff.* The word "for" was also highlighted in red. As soft breezes blew through her office's tall, open windows, Lew mulled over the message, thinking less about the bumper sticker than about how being elected sheriff of the county could change her life. Did she really want to go there?

Before she could take the leap to nod her approval to the campaign manager seated in front of her, the phone on her desk rang.

"Chief," said Marlaine on Dispatch, "we got an emergency call from Bud Tillman, the manager at Sweo's. Some kids just ambushed a guy they insist is a sexual predator. Bud says you know one of the kids—Doc Osborne's granddaughter, Mason. Want me to send Officer Adamczak?"

Lew looked up from her phone. Mason's mother was standing in front of her: Erin Amundson, her campaign manager.

"Thanks, Marlaine, but I'll handle it," said Lew, rising to her feet. "Did Bud say if the kids are still there?"

"Yes, he won't let them leave. The guy they tried to stop drove off though."

"Tell Bud I'm on my way."

"Meeting over?" asked Erin, watching Lew.

"Yes and no," said Lew. "You better come with me. You may have a new client—your daughter."

# Chapter Two

The four kids sat squeezed together on a bench in the store manager's office. Standing in front of the manager's desk, her arms folded, Lew studied the four faces that kept sneaking looks at each other. Nervous grins flashed and disappeared. As she had encouraged Erin not to say anything to her daughter until after Lew had talked with them, Mason's mom stood quietly in a corner off to one side of the desk.

Larry Fortran, tallest of the four, sat with his shoulders hunched as one bony knee jiggled with impatience. Lew sensed that he was ready to argue they hadn't done anything wrong. Next to him was short, round-faced Denny Wayne, whose piercing black eyes reminded Lew of an enterprising chipmunk. The minute his mother walked in, his expression changed from wise guy to stricken. So stricken that if he'd been fifty years older she would have been worried he was on the verge of a heart attack. No doubt he was panicked over what was going to happen when he got home.

John Mayer sat beside Mason, pretending to be calm. Lew guessed him to be the mastermind behind their caper. She knew his father, a real-estate appraiser more than once suspected of taking bribes to inflate property values—and a man known to consider himself the smartest guy in the room. *Maybe he is*, thought Lew. *He hasn't been caught yet.* John took after his mother, who had discovered her error early in her marriage and divorced the "real-estate expert." John was a too-bright, serious kid.

And then there was Mason, tall for her age and slender, with the high cheekbones and dusky complexion of her Metis grandfather, whose great-grandmother was an Ojibwa from Quebec married to a French-Canadian fur trader. Lew was surprised every time she saw Mason alongside her mother: Erin had a porcelain complexion and wore her honey-blonde hair in a long braid.

Contemplating the fidgeting four young people, Lew was well aware that she was facing a complex situation, the immediate issue being that Mason's mother was managing her campaign for county sheriff. And then there was Mason's grandfather, who played more than a modest role in Lew's life.

\* \* \*

After retiring from his full-time dental practice, Dr. Paul—"Doc"—Osborne had pursued a long-time goal to become an odontologist, a forensic dental expert.

Since he was the only forensic dental expert in the region, both the Loon Lake police and the Wausau crime lab relied on his expertise for identifying dead and decomposing bodies.

Doc Osborne was also a student of Lew's—in the trout stream. They had connected three years earlier when he signed up for fly-casting lessons only to discover that the male (he assumed) instructor named "Lou" was in fact "Lew"— Lewellyn Ferris, the Loon Lake chief of police, an expert fly fisherman who enjoyed teaching people how to cast a fly rod and other basics of fly fishing on the side.

That first meeting had led from a teacher–student relationship to a friendship, a very close friendship. Or as Doc, a widower, liked to describe it, "she keeps refusing to marry me." Then he grins.

*　*　*

Lew cast an inner sigh. Yes, she was looking at a complex situation. With a shrug, she decided not to worry about it. No law was being broken by letting four preteens know they were lucky to have avoided what might have been a dangerous confrontation. With that decision, she came up with a plan.

She walked over to where Erin was standing. Lew shared her idea and Erin responded with enthusiasm. "This is needed," she said, "I'm happy to find the right person and get this under way ASAP." Erin herself was "the right person" to find an authority on the legal issues involved. A lawyer who specialized in wills and probate, she was married to Loon Lake's district attorney. She also strove to parent three challenging children.

"Thank you," said Lew with a mild sense of relief. She walked back to the front of the desk. "All right," she said, "which of you wants to tell me exactly what happened here this afternoon?"

Three heads turned to John.

"We were making a citizens' arrest," said John, his voice cracking with preadolescent stress.

"And why would that be?" she asked the foursome.

John checked the faces of his friends before answering, "Chief Ferris, that man we tried to stop—he's a sexual predator. He saw Mason's picture online and texted that he wants to date her. She told him she's only twelve, but he said he was okay with that. Chief Ferris," the boy's voice rose, cracking, "he's twenty-four years old. Isn't that criminal?"

"We looked it up," volunteered Larry, "that violates age of consent laws. And—and—" Larry's voice shook with emotion, "he tried to bribe her to run away with him. Tell the chief, Mason. Tell her what he tried to do."

The kids were sitting up straight now, tense. "He said he'd buy me an iPhone if I went to SummerFest with him," said Mason.

"A-a-and . . ." Larry stuttered as he interrupted, "that would be an overnight trip. Right? All the way to Milwaukee!" Heads nodded, bodies squirmed, and Denny fell off the bench.

"Take it easy, guys," said Lew, raising both hands to calm them down. "Yes, I hear what you're saying. I understand. What did you say to that, Mason?"

"Well," said Mason, "I didn't really say anything. I texted him that we could talk about it. That's why he said he wanted to meet me here today. We'd talk about it."

"But that's not all he said," John pushed his way back into the conversation. "He wanted to show you his bed, right?"

"His bed?" Lew asked, stunned.

"His bed?" Erin stepped forward from the back of the room, her face pale with alarm.

"Yes," said John, looking toward Mason for confirmation. "He said he could make up a bed in the back of his big SUV so they could drive all night and get there in time to see Taylor Swift."

"Oh, my God," said Erin. "Chief—"

Lew raised her hand again, this time to quiet the frantic mother.

"This is all I need to know right now, kids," she said. "I'll take it from here. Oh wait, one more thing. How did he happen to find you, Mason?"

"My picture was on the TV news a couple weeks ago 'cause I caught that big northern ice fishing with Grandpa.

Remember? It was the biggest one caught all winter. So the guy started texting me after that. . . ."

"Mason told all of us about him, and that's when we all thought maybe we should trap him before he hurts any one," said John, a hint of pride in his voice.

"I see," said Lew. "All right, you four. No more citizens' arrest attempts, understand? If you see or know of something wrong happening, you call the Loon Lake police. Understood? We are trained to handle situations like this. You're not, and you could get hurt. Now I want you and your parents in my office at five thirty this afternoon to discuss this further. Are we clear?"

"I have tennis practice," said Denny.

"You *had* tennis practice," said Lew. "Be there with your folks."

The four exchanged anxious looks.

"All right, you can leave now." Lew watched four twelve-year-olds move faster than they probably had in a year. When they were gone, she turned to Erin.

"That was a close call," said Lew. "Are you okay?"

"Not sure," said Erin. "I just . . . it's so hard to protect kids these days. Your idea to get a professional in to talk to these kids—all the middle-schoolers—is excellent. Who knows who the next target . . . " A tear slid down her cheek but she wiped it away. "Is there anything more terrifying for a parent?"

"We're lucky these are pretty smart kids," said Lew. "I don't excuse what they did, but at least Mason wasn't . . ." She didn't finish her sentence. "Erin," she said, "I will see that that man never sets foot in Loon Lake again. There are laws against what he did."

"I know that." Erin sighed, "still . . ." She shrugged as she walked around the desk, a grim look on her face. She paused at the door leading out of the manager's office.

"Chief, you never said if that bumper sticker is okay. I think it's well done, easy to read from a distance. We need to order it right away if that's okay with you." Lew could hear her trying to perk up her spirits.

"Fine with me," said Lew though she still wondered if she was making the right decision—on running for office, that is.

\* \* \*

Stopping to thank Bud, the manager, for how he'd handled the situation with the kids, she asked, "Any idea who that fellow was?"

"Oh, yeah, that's Noah McDonough, son of Grace McDonough. You know who she is—the one who refuses to let the county change the name of Toad Lake even though we've got sixty-seven property owners, including me, who have petitioned to change it to White Pine Lake. We've even offered to call it McDonough Lake for God's sake, but that old—woman," he caught himself before using an expletive, "won't budge."

"I did hear something about that," said Lew, remembering that a colleague on the county board had mentioned the local dispute. "But hasn't it been Toad Lake since like the eighteen hundreds? Why change it now?"

Bud snorted in disgust. "Who wants to stay at a resort on lovely Toad Lake? Hold a wedding reception on bee-u-ti-ful Toad Lake? But, hey, Grace owns eighty percent of the land around the lake, and she won't budge. I guess when you're worth millions you get to call the shots. But why on earth wouldn't she want a change? It's a lovely lake."

"C'mon, Bud," said Lew managing a grin. "Toads aren't all bad. They eat mosquitoes, don't they?"

# Chapter Three

❧

While she waited to receive the warrant she needed before confronting the individual identified by the store manager, Lew stopped by her office to get a copy of the county plat book. A quick study showed the McDonough Trust property to be less than half an hour from where Lew had been parked in front of Sweo's market. It also showed that the trust owned not only the largest percentage of shoreline bordering Toad Lake but significant shoreline to the east along the Pelican River, a prized waterway for walleye, musky, bass—and daredevil kayakers.

Lew was impressed. Grace McDonough was sitting on the kind of land that had made descendants of the timber barons in the 1880s very wealthy people.

\* \* \*

The entrance to the McDonough residence was marked by two crumbling stone pillars over which, sculpted in wrought iron, was the name McDonough. An elegant entrance, though the paved road beyond it—like the pillars—needed work.

"Haven't seen one of those in a while," thought Lew as she drove by an old white frame house with broken windows and a sagging front porch. The abandoned house, likely considered a "mansion" in its day, surprised her, as most people inheriting classic wood-frame structures from the early 1900s tended to restore them, often having them declared "historic" and taking care to be sure any restoration was true to the era.

Down the road, past an old barn and around a curve, was the answer to why the old place was abandoned: a red-cedar contemporary jutted out over a small inlet of what had to be Toad Lake. As the house was windowed from the ground up to its flat metal roof, Lew speculated that the owner must be a summer resident with an architect from the Deep South, both of whom were ignorant of life in a northern Wisconsin winter.

She pulled into one of five parking spaces to the left of the house. The parking area fronted a garage large enough to hold at least four vehicles. A black Range Rover was parked there, its license plate matching the number that Larry Fortran had handed her.

A short walkway from the garage ended in a ramp that ran up to a deck on the front of the main building. Lew walked across the deck to a screen door. A heavy oak door just inside it stood open. Hearing a mix of male and female voices inside but unable to make out what they were saying, Lew reached for the carved loon that passed for a doorbell and waited. Up close she noticed that the red-cedar exterior could use a good staining.

A figure appeared on the other side of the screen door, a pudgy woman wearing a loose white shirt over tan capris, her streaked blonde hair pulled back into a pony-tail. She looked surprised to see someone in a police uni-form. "Yeah? What?" Her tone was defensive. "I paid the property tax yesterday. It's taken care of, okay?" She moved to close the interior door.

Lew stuck her foot out to hold the door open. "Mrs. McDonough? I'm not the county clerk. I'm Chief Lewellyn Ferris of the Loon Lake Police Department."

"Ms. McDonough," said the woman, interrupting her. "There is no Mister. Why?"

Ignoring her belligerence, Lew said, "May I come in, please? I'm looking for Noah McDonough. I believe that's his car parked outside. May I speak with him, please?"

As her tone made it clear this wasn't a request but an order, confusion spread across the woman's face.

"You mean my son?"

"If he's Noah McDonough," said Lew, "yes, I'm look-ing for that individual. Is he here?"

"Noah!" The woman kept her eyes on Lew as she bel-lowed in a voice sure to travel across Toad Lake and back.

"Noah, what the hell is this about?"

As she spoke a young man no taller than his mother but much slimmer came around the corner. He had short brown hair brushed straight up on his head so it stood in points. Lew recognized it as a style worn by the young musicians who played at local music events across the Northwoods. He was holding a sandwich in one hand.

"Noah McDonough, you're under arrest for violating Wisconsin Age of Consent Law and intent to kidnap or otherwise harm a minor." Lew proceeded to read him his rights. "Please hand over your smartphone."

"Tell me that again?" asked Grace McDonough.

Lew gave a short description of her son's texting, the iPhone offer, and the potential use of the Range Rover for a trip south with an underage girl. Then repeated her request: "Hand over your smartphone and any other cell or smartphones belonging to you."

"An iPhone? You were going to buy her an iPhone? Where the hell did you get the money?" The woman turned on her son. "Told you this morning no more Amazon orders."

She was so unconcerned over the seriousness of her son's attempting to entice an underage child that Lew wondered if this had happened before. And how many times? If so, why wasn't Noah McDonough a registered sex offender?

Noah stared at the floor, refusing to answer his mother.

"All right," said Grace, sounding irritated, as if this was just one more inconvenience in her day. "I'll call our lawyer."

She gave Lew a withering glance, "I don't think you know who we are. I'm Grace McDonough, and my family has been coming here for three generations. My father paid for your damn hospital! What you are doing is inexcusable and I'm going to sue . . . how can you be sure those kids aren't lying?"

Before Lew could say a word, she went on, "Noah is not the kind of person who does such a thing—you're looking at someone with a master's in business administration from the University of Illinois. He's not stupid."

"They have your son on video in their phones," said Lew. "The four young people who saw and heard him are willing to testify to what he attempted to do." She didn't add that having an MBA did not prevent a person from being a bad actor.

"Oh, right," said the woman dismissively. "I've heard this before. Don't worry, Noah, I'll meet you in town at the police station with our lawyer and take care of this."

Noah had still not said anything other than confirming his name. Now he asked, "Do you have to handcuff me?"

"Yes, you'll be riding to the station with me right now," said Lew.

\* \* \*

Minutes later, as she was closing the rear door of her cruiser, a white pickup drove into one of the parking places. Blue letters on the side of the truck read "Normandy Mining and Exploration."

As Lew backed and turned to go down the driveway, she saw the driver of the pickup talking with Grace at the top of the walkway to the house. She couldn't help wondering: Could Grace McDonough be opening her land to the company looking to do sulfide mining in the Northwoods? That would make some people very, very unhappy—especially if the land bordered the Pelican River.

# Chapter Four

Grace McDonough did not appear at the police station until twenty minutes before Lew had planned to meet with the parents of the four students. When she did show up, she walked straight into Lew's office before the front desk could alert Lew she had arrived.

"Where's my son?" she said, both hands planted on her hips, a belligerent look on her face.

"Your son will be held here until I can arrange for a bond hearing tomorrow or Thursday," said Lew. "We have a call in to the county judge to arrange to get on the schedule. I'll call you as soon as we know."

"That's BS," said the woman. "I know the judge. I talked to the judge, and I'm taking Noah home. *Right. Now.*"

Lew knew influence when she saw it. No surprise. A man she recognized from court hearings in nearby Oneida County appeared to be trying to hide behind his client. It wasn't difficult: Grace was short and wide and he was short and spindly.

Repressing a smile at the performance taking place in front of her, Lew picked up her phone and called the warden. "Please bring Noah McDonough to my office." She set the phone down and looked at her guests.

"Please, Ms. McDonough, won't you and your lawyer take a seat while we wait?" She pointed to the chairs in front of her desk.

"I'll do no such thing," said Grace sputtered. "You have my son here on a bogus charge and I'm not going anywhere without him." She threw an angry look on the lawyer.

"I have four witnesses to Mr. Noah McDonough's attempts to entice an underage female," said Lew, handing the lawyer the written document that detailed the contents of the e-mails Noah had sent Mason Amundson, age twelve.

After reading through the material, the lawyer pulled Grace over to one corner of the room and whispered to her. Grace remonstrated, her body quivering with anger, and he whispered some more. With a loud expletive, Grace slammed her purse on the floor.

"Ooh, I hope you don't have your phone in there," said the lawyer, cringing.

A knock on the door indicated that the warden had arrived with Noah. Grace ran toward her son, arms open and ready to embrace him, but Noah put up both hands and shoved her away. "Stop it, Mom. Just make bail for me will ya? I hate it here."

"Okay, okay, settle down, son. Everything's under control," said the lawyer, stepping between mother and son.

While Grace bent over Lew's desk to sign the legal document freeing her son until he was due for the bond hearing in court, Lew studied Noah. She would never have guessed him to be twenty-four years old.

Standing with shoulders hunched and a pout on his face, which showed signs of acne, he looked more like a teenager than a young adult. And he was so pale, which made him look even younger. A bizarre thought crossed Lew's mind: no wonder the guy had tried to date a twelve-year-old—he looked about that age himself.

The lawyer took a moment to review the document Grace had signed, then nodded. In less than a minute he was able to usher mother and son out the door. Before he closed the door behind the three of them, he threw Lew a look of apology, then grimaced and left.

\*   \*   \*

"What else is on that phone?" Nancy Fortran's question rang out despite the fact Lew's office was crowded with the four kids, four adults, herself, and Officer Todd Donovan, whom she'd asked to join them, as he had a son the same age as Mason and her friends.

Along with John's father, Larry and Denny's mothers were there, as was Erin. Each youngster sat next to his parent around the long, low table under the tall windows at the far end of Lew's office. At the moment, Nancy Fortran was on her feet, punching the air with the index finger of her right hand.

Lew wasn't surprised. The woman often showed up at meetings of the Loon Lake City Council, where she would rage, accusing council members of doing their best to ruin Loon Lake's business community. No one ever called Nancy "quiet."

The daughter and granddaughter of men who had built the largest insurance agency north of Wausau, Nancy had adopted her father's bombastic mannerisms when she took it over, managing to humiliate new hires to the degree that employees rarely lasted more than six months working for her.

"Yeah," she repeated, waving the finger of authority, "how the hell many other kids has that man corrupted? How many pictures of our children are being violated on the Internet? How many—"

Lew interrupted her: "Those are all good questions, Mrs. Fortran. Dani Wright, our IT expert, has his phone and is tracking the e-mails and photos. She's found no evidence yet that Noah McDonough has approached any other young people in our community. He just returned to his mother's summer home from college, so we can feel confident . . ."

"Well, I'm not confident, Chief Ferris." Nancy spat out the words. "You don't know the Internet these days. I want the FBI in on this. Now. Right. Now."

Lew gave her a long look before saying, "Thank you, I'll look into that." She turned to John's father, who had tried to interrupt. "Mr. Mayer, you look like you have something to say."

Stanley Mayer was the closest to a walrus that Lew had ever met. Become a real-estate appraiser after having failed as a stockbroker, he was large man given to sporting strange mustaches. He had a deep, sonorous voice with which he made profound—at least to him—statements.

Today was no exception. "I differ with Nancy," he said in his sepulchral voice as he rose to his feet, his ample stomach hanging over the edge of the conference table. "Grace McDonough is an outstanding member of our summer community. You know she lives full-time in Palm Springs, California, right? And she donates a small fortune to our local hospital, which her grandfather founded—thousands of dollars annually."

He looked around the room for confirmation of that crucial fact. "She is not going to allow her son to hurt anyone. This was a prank. That's all—a boyish prank."

"Excuse me, Stanley," said Lew. "When did being wealthy mean that people behave the way they should? Or let me ask you another question. Is Grace McDonough one of your clients?"

All she got from Stanley was a sheepish look and a shrug as he sat down, crossed his right leg over the left, and started pumping his right foot.

"All right, time for good news and bad news," said Lew. "We'll start with the good news." She beckoned to Erin, who stood up. "Mrs. Amundson—I believe you all know Mason's mother, and I'm sure you know she is a well-respected lawyer in our community. At my request she has spoken with a mental health expert who specializes in coaching middle and high-school-age boys and girls on how to deal with online stalking and potential sexual predators. Erin, please take it from here."

Lew watched as Erin took the time to make eye contact with each parent and child. She detailed the credentials of the expert who was due to arrive from Madison in two days and who would teach a series of classes at both the middle school and the high school.

As she finished describing the nature of the classes, she added, "We want to teach our children how to be safe—but, equally important, how to be kind, compassionate."

Lew saw Nancy tilt her head, questioning.

"Yes, compassionate," said Erin. "We want them to understand that the person who is guilty of predatory behavior is not a well person. He has serious mental health problems and needs help. Professional help.

"If our students understand that, they will be quicker to report any suspicious behavior they may encounter whether online or in person. Some kids hold back because they feel they did something to cause the stalker's behavior. This approach helps young people to not feel guilty, to know that an individual who approaches them is someone who needs help. It's a good way to teach compassion."

Lew caught the stony expressions on the faces of Nancy Fortran and Stanley Mayer. When it came to those two, compassion was not their long suit. But Denny's mother, Lara, understood what Erin was saying. She gave a nod of support and hugged her son.

"Back to you, Chief Ferris," said Erin, sitting down next to Mason.

"Thanks, Erin," said Lew. She stood up. "Now the bad news . . ."

The room was quiet. Lew crossed her arms and walked back and forth in front of the conference table, her eyes down studying the floor.

Looking up and keeping her voice even, she said, "This is for you—John, Denny, Larry, Mason—yes, you scared that guy. But you may not scare the next one. Kids, the man I arrested is someone who knew he was breaking the law. People like that can be dangerous, more dangerous than you can imagine.

"You may not realize it, but the text messages you sent him can be traced to your phone, and your phone location can be traced. What I'm trying to say is someone like that can find you and find you—any one of you—when you are alone. Do you hear me?"

Four heads nodded.

"Do you promise not to do this again? And promise that you will attend every one of the classes that Mrs. Amundson is setting up?"

Four heads nodded. All four twelve-year-olds looked terrified.

Lew felt a glimmer of relief. Only a glimmer. She couldn't be sure they wouldn't do it again. They were twelve.

# Chapter Five

⌒

Sitting at Doc's kitchen table while he sliced an avocado to add to the tossed salad he had made to go with the spaghetti, Lew gave him a detailed account of how his granddaughter and her three buddies had attempted a citizen's arrest.

"I'm impressed," said Osborne when she had finished. "Sounds like Mason is a natural for law enforcement." He grinned.

Lew did not. "That's not funny. Those kids have no idea how dangerous a situation like that can be."

Osborne set the salad bowl on the table and reached over to rub her shoulders. "You're right. I spoke without thinking. But that Mason! I can just see that kid coming up with a crazy plan like that." He shook his head. "Too smart for her own good."

"Takes after her grandfather?" Lew winked and served herself some salad. It had been a long day, and this was one of those nights she was happy not to have to cook.

*   *   *

Osborne recalled that it had been three years since he had signed up for a lesson on how to cast the fly rod he'd kept hidden from his late wife. Mary Lee had married him knowing full well that he loved living in the Northwoods so he could practice dentistry and have his Wednesdays off to fish musky. Or, as he joked with his buddies—not Mary Lee—that he practiced dentistry so he could afford to fish.

She must have thought she could change him because she spent the next thirty years of their marriage accusing him of "fishing all the damn time" and saying, "You spend all that money on fishing poles and other crap instead of decent furniture for the living room."

That was not true. He had made sure his wife could always have what she wanted for the house, for her clothes, for their daughters, and for a new car every two years. Still, she never forgave him for passing up an opportunity to buy a practice in Milwaukee—"where you could have made decent money for a change, Paul," he remembered her telling him. After her death, he had unearthed the rod from where he had hidden it at the back of the cupboard holding rakes and shovels in the garage. At last he could give fly-fishing, a sport he had long admired, a try.

The owner of Ralph's Sporting Goods had recommended an instructor good with beginners, a woman who moonlighted teaching fly-fishing when not on duty with the Loon Lake police. Shortly after they met that day Lew's boss died unexpectedly and the Loon Lake City Council promoted her to chief of police. Fortunately for Osborne, she continued her coaching in the trout stream, which led to an interesting development in both their lives. While she proved to be a fine instructor in the art of fly casting, Osborne brought an unexpected talent to that relationship too.

Though he had recently retired from his dental practice of thirty years, he had not retired a personal fascination with the developing field of dental forensics. Within months of meeting Lew, two things happened: he upgraded his fly rod and casting skill, while she tapped into his expertise for identifying the living and the dead thanks to the irrefutable evidence furnished by teeth. Nor did it hurt that local secrets hidden in Osborne's dental files, which he had stashed in a secret room at the back of his fishing shed—in defiance of Mary Lee's demand that he destroy them and "not clutter up our house"—had proved invaluable in the solving of more than one murder when, at the request of the police department and the Wausau Crime Lab, he had checked the files and discovered information that advanced the investigation.

\* \* \*

Helping herself to a healthy portion of spaghetti, Lew said, "Doc, you've been living in Loon Lake long enough to know more of the local history than I do. What's the story behind Grace McDonough? That son of hers is rather odd. He doesn't say much, certainly looks younger than twenty-four. Any siblings, or is he an only child?"

"Don't get me started on Grace," said Osborne scooping noodles onto his plate. "How do you like my sauce? Made it with ground venison."

"Sauce is excellent. Back to Grace. Doesn't sound like she's one of your favorites."

"Her mother would bring her to the office during the summers not long after I took over my dad's practice," said Osborne. "She was a sullen teenager in those days. Years later, after she had that son of hers, what's his name?"

"Noah."

"Right. I only saw him once. I think he was just five or six at the time. She brought him in with a broken tooth and when I leaned over to examine the kid, he bit me. And he let out a piercing scream as if I'd bitten him!" Osborne laughed at the memory.

"So Grace rushes in from the waiting room where I had insisted she wait and she starts to read me the riot act. Quite a command of the English language that woman. That was too much for this gentleman. I got that kid out of the dental chair and both of them out the door so fast. Sent them over to poor Metternich. He cursed me out later." Osborne smiled.

"But he's sent me a few bad ones over the years too." He swirled a bite of spaghetti around his fork, then said, "Haven't seen the boy since. Glimpsed Grace once or twice at the bars back when I was drinking."

Osborne grimaced, no doubt remembering his own sordid battle with the bottle. "She was known to slam a few down in those days. Other than that all I know is from my friend Herm who's on the County Board and complains that she shows up and tries to throw her weight around. They have to listen to her since her old man endowed the hospital. But I only hear about that over coffee at McDonald's. Most people I know try to avoid the woman."

"So she didn't really grow up here?"

"No. Summer people." He swirled the spaghetti again and Lew waited. She could tell a story was coming. A good story from the twinkle in Osborne's eyes.

"Her father was quite the man about town. We all knew it, and his special friend was no secret. Gloria Bertrand was her name. A voluptuous gal. She was the local hairdresser."

Osborne gave a slight smile. "Rumor was that when the old man died and the widow had a memorial service at their place out there on Toad Lake, Gloria showed up."

"You're kidding."

"She didn't go near the family but was standing close enough that Grace's mother saw her, grabbed a shotgun from inside that old house they had, and threatened to shoot her if she ever laid foot on their property again. People still talk about it. And there's more. Gloria never owned up to who Stanley's father was. The story is that Stanley Mayer is his illegitimate son. All anyone in Loon Lake ever knew was that right after the old man passed away of a heart attack—he wasn't that old, maybe in his early sixties—Gloria went off to beauty school in Green Bay and came back a few months later clearly pregnant. She insisted she had gotten married over in Green Bay but divorced the father right after she got pregnant."

"You think Stanley knows that?"

"Not sure anyone has ever been so unkind as to tell him, and who knows what Gloria told him."

"He can certainly find out, don't you think?" said Lew. "What with Ancestry and all these DNA tracers that could be easy."

"Well, old man McDonough was quite the charmer, Lew. Who knows how many offspring he had? Has, I should say."

"Was he ever a patient?"

"Oh, yes, and his wife—patients of my dad's. Both Grace's parents were very pleasant people when they were in the office. Grace is the wild card. Always has been."

Osborne savored a big bite of his spaghetti, then put his fork down and wiped his mouth with his napkin.

"You know, Lew, I have always wondered who Noah's father was. No one's ever said, which is odd. Very odd. From what I recall of Grace's mother, she was quite proper, the type who would have given her daughter the most expensive, elaborate wedding their money could buy. Know what I mean?"

Lew did, thinking to herself, *like your wife did for your daughter, Mallory. And a lot of good that did for Mallory's marriage.* But she kept the thought to herself.

"This is a lot of fatherless sons, Doc," said Lew with a stab at her own spaghetti.

* * *

After the dishes were done, they settled in to watch the local news. This was Lew's favorite time of the evenings she spent at Doc's, a feeling that never failed to surprise her.

During the years before the fateful day they had met in the trout stream, their lives had intersected on occasion, but never in a remarkable way. After all, Loon Lake had a population slightly over thirteen hundred, so knowing the person in line ahead of you at the Loon Lake market was not unusual.

Before he arrived for instruction that day, Lew had known Doc under two very different circumstances: as the young dentist to whom she took her two children every fall for their school check-ups—and shortly after joining the Loon Lake police force she had arrested him for drunken driving.

Unhappy though his thirty-year marriage had been (something Lew learned from his close friend and neighbor, Ray Pradt), when he lost his wife Osborne had lost his bearings. With no one to bully him into showing up on time for meals and manage life's other daily rituals, he found himself so desperately lonely that he reached for the bottle and nearly killed himself. Only an intervention run by his daughters, who checked him into Minnesota's Hazelden Betty Ford Rehab Foundation, saved his life. He was early into recovery when he stumbled on that fly rod and followed the urge that put in him in a stream on a summer day that would change his life—and his instructor's.

Now, three years into their relationship, they had negotiated a pleasant compromise: two nights a week at Doc's home on Loon Lake and two nights at her little farmhouse out on tiny Silver Bass Lake, which Doc insisted on calling a "pond," and three nights on their own. Whoever hosted did the cooking and also took care of the dishes. And they rarely missed the ten o'clock news. A comfortable mixture of time together, time apart.

And every night when Lew settled in with Osborne on the sofa, she would consider again, as she had that first day, how good-looking he was—tall and slim, with a full head of black hair graying at the temples. How pleasant he was to be around: his dark eyes twinkling with natural good humor and his quiet air of authority. Not only did she love looking at him, but his calm, thoughtful voice made her world seem not so worrisome. What had his late wife been thinking?

Lew was lucky and she knew it. Doc kept saying he was the lucky one, but she knew better. Though he had brought up marriage—insisting his adult daughters would be shocked that "their old man is living in sin"— Lew had laughed. After her own marriage at eighteen to a cute high school crush who turned into a cute irresponsible drunk had ended in divorce, she had vowed that so long as she could support herself she would never marry again. So life was good, and if she were to be elected county sheriff in the coming election, she would be able to support herself well indeed.

\* \* \*

"Time for the news," said Osborne, walking into the living room and wiping his hands on the kitchen towel as he turned on the television. Lew set aside the report on the arrest of Noah McDonough that she had been reviewing and made room for him beside her on the couch.

The evening news opened with a report of the arrest of the younger McDonough and a brief description of how four "juveniles" had set a trap for the "assumed sexual predator."

"You're right, Lewellyn," said Osborne after the newscast was over. "That was not smart of those youngsters."

"We are so lucky nothing worse happened," said Lew. "Lesson learned. By the time the kids and all their friends finish the classes that Erin is setting up, I think they will all be very, very careful."

A break in the news for advertising had Osborne reaching for the "mute" button when a familiar figure appeared on the screen. "Hold on," said Lew, putting a hand on his arm, "don't mute it."

On the screen was a striking image: Bert Flynn, her adversary in the race to replace Sheriff Gary Moore. He was dressed for deer hunting, which made sense as a huge twelve-point buck crowded into the image too. The trophy buck was hanging from the branch of a tree as a man's voice intoned: "Vote Bert Flynn for McBride County Sheriff. We deserve a man's man." Osborne hit the mute.

"Gee, that's subtle," said Lew, throwing down her file of documents. "Too bad they don't mention he's twenty-six years old with two years of experience."

"Take it easy," said Osborne. "You're the first woman in this region to be named chief of police, you have a stellar record of crime solving over the past three years, and you are going to be the first woman elected sheriff of McBride County."

"But I don't have a photo with a twelve-point buck, dammit."

"True," said Osborne, musing. "You think this hunting issue has traction?"

Lew drew herself up and deepened her voice, "It's manly."

"More manly than fly-fishing?"

"This is really about guns, Doc. People don't picture women with guns and guns imply law enforcement. Pretty simple."

"Okay. You hunt. You beat me hands down when we went bird hunting last fall. Didn't we take a photo of you with that grouse you got with the twenty-gauge you inherited from your grandfather?"

Lew gazed at him for a long moment. "Yes, we did, and I look good in it if I say so myself."

"Dig it out. We'll show it to Erin. Isn't she working with that PR guy from the TV station on an ad for you?"

"She is now." Lew jumped to her feet. "But I need a good line to counter that 'manly man' routine."

"*No crime has gone unsolved since Chief Lewellyn Ferris took charge.* Then we get a couple of the people whose lives you've saved to give testimonials. My granddaughter Beth for one. You saved her from the drug addict creep who kidnapped her. And me—I have a few things I can say—"

"No, Doc." Lew laughed. "You have a conflict of interest. But these are good ideas, and I'll work with Erin and the public relations guy at the station."

"Just remember, Lewellyn: one live human beats a twelve-point buck."

# Chapter Six

It was five thirty in the morning as the man picked his way, stumbling and sliding, down the rock-strewn incline toward the marshy hummock hugging the shoreline.

"Dammit," he cursed silently. "I gotta have cataract surgery before I kill myself doing this." He sidestepped, leaning into the hill as he got closer to the nest.

At four in the morning he'd been awakened by a buzzing on his smart watch; one of the trail cameras had clicked on. He rushed out to the garage to check the video but there was nothing moving on the screen. Not even the loons. He went back to bed, but he couldn't sleep. The loon family was like his own: the parents were his siblings, their chicks his youngsters. He knew it was crazy, but he'd been watching the parents for fifteen years now. Seven times they had had chicks and most had survived, but when two were stolen by the bald eagle he had felt like his own children had been killed.The trail cameras were his weapons against the marauders. The investment had been costly enough—between the Apple watch and the six cameras—that he had hidden the total expense from his wife. He had rigged them close to the ground and overhead, and, so far, success. At least for this hatch. At least so far.

By five AM he gave up, got dressed, whispered to his wife he was leaving and drove to the lake as quickly as he could, hoping all the way that nothing terrible had happened.

Loon parents keep their young in the nest for a good twelve weeks, a dangerous time when the loon family is a prime target for predators like fishers and fox and bald eagles. Though loons may live thirty years, they have few offspring, for one simple reason: they lose their young ones to the evil stalkers lurking in the bushes, creeping along the shoreline, attacking from the treetops.

The man pulled out his notebook, recorded the date, then forced himself to pause and peer through the tag alders protecting the nest. Whew. Both chicks were there. One parent was gone, likely gathering breakfast. He relaxed. A rustling in the brush behind him, likely a raccoon from the sound of it, did not divert his attention. The family couldn't be hurt now—not with him there to shoo any invader away.

The thump on the back of his neck sent him flying forward, over the tag alders and into the mud alongside the nest. Another blow and he lay still. From the back, he appeared to be facedown in the water: if he wasn't dead already, he would drown.

At five forty-five a wooden rowboat came drifting along, staying just outside the weeds near the shoreline. The boat held two fishermen, one rowing and one standing in the front of the boat casting in silence so as not to disturb the walleyes they hoped were hiding among the branches of the dead trees that had toppled into the water.

"Oh my god, do you see that?" the man standing at the front of the boat shouted to his partner. "See the body over there? Call 911!"

"What's the location?" asked his partner.

"Tell 'em it's on the west side of Lynn Lake just north of the public landing. Maybe half a mile up."

When he could see the water was only knee deep, the fisherman let himself out of the boat. He waded over to where the man was lying near a loon nest and was relieved to see that his face was not in the water.

He touched the man's neck. "Got a pulse! Call 911 again. Tell 'em to meet us there. Hand me our life jackets."

Turning the man gently onto his back, the fisherman slipped the life jackets under his body and pushed him along in the shallow water. By the time they had reached the boat landing, the ambulance was waiting and two EMTs waded out to help carry the victim in to shore.

# Chapter Seven

Lew woke to a cup of hot coffee being handed to her by the man whose face she loved seeing first thing in the morning. Like watching the evening news, their mornings also had a ritual. A breeze off the lake would drift in through the open bedroom window, and Doc would sit beside her with his mug of hot coffee while they discussed each one's plans for the day. She would be preparing for reports of drunk drivers, gas-station break-ins, domestic disturbances, and drug busts—the usual. He would soon be off to McDonald's for two more cups of coffee with his buddies to discuss the state of the universe—and maybe some local gossip.

More than once, Doc's coffee crowd had proved invaluable to Lew. The men were all longtime residents of Loon Lake. One, like Osborne, was a retired dentist; another had owned the local newspaper; a third had run the town's only accounting business; and three had been managers at either the paper mill or its printing operation. Two of the men, like Osborne, were widowed, one divorced, and the rest in long-term wearying (according to them) marriages. All were hunters and fishermen. In short, it was a crowd that fancied themselves as knowing everything about Loon Lake—the good, the bad, and the disquieting.

So it was that Lew and Doc's early-morning cups of coffee were treasured by both: a lovely start to the day. Or, as she said to her daughter when explaining why she split her week between her place and his: "Why not? Doc feels just like home."

*　*　*

By six fifteen that Wednesday morning, Loon Lake Chief of Police Lewellyn Ferris was headed to her office and slowing at a sharp turn just a mile down the road from Doc's place, a good move, as a young fawn darted across the town road in front of her. She smiled as the lithe creature disappeared into a stand of new growth pine.

"'Morning," she said as she approached Marlaine, the dispatcher on the morning shift. Leaning over the counter in front of Marlaine, she grimaced as she asked, "What's our bad news for today?" Bad news translated to too much paperwork.

"Dani must have something," said Marlaine. "Girl was here when I got in at six. When was the last time that happened?" Marlaine grinned. Lew headed down the hall past Dani's cubicle.

"Chief," Dani jumped up from where she was sitting in front of a computer and followed Lew into her office. "Got news on that McDonough case that you'll want to follow up on ASAP."

"More stalking?" Lew sat down at her desk and turned on her own computer.

"Yes, but not here—out in Palm Springs where he was living with his mother. I've downloaded the report for you. But here's the issue. I think he should be registered here as a sex offender. Isn't that the law?"

"Yes, they call them 'travelers' and they should be registered," said Lew. "Good work. Anything else on Noah's phone? More photos of other young girls? That warrant allows us to search everything on the phone."

"No. I'm still checking on phone numbers that I located. So far they appear to be friends and some from his mother."

Shortly before noon, the dispatcher rang Lew's desk phone, "Chief, you have an emergency call. Family. I'm putting it through."

"Lewellyn," said the female voice, sounding frantic. "Pete's dead." It was her sister-in-law, Linda.

"What? How?" Lew jumped to her feet.

"I dunno. They just called."

"Who called?"

"The EMTs. A fisherman found his body by that nest of loons he's been keeping an eye on. Heart attack. I told him he was eating too many eggs . . ."

"Where is he now?"

"Emergency room at St. Mary's."

"I'm on my way." Lew put the phone down and ran.

Linda was Pete's second wife and one of Lew's least favorite people. Not unlike Doc, her brother had been lonely after his first wife died of breast cancer. Unfortunately—and differently from Osborne—he had married the first woman who paid him attention. Lew had wanted to point out that she was more likely paying attention to his retirement account, but she knew that wouldn't be wise—or kind. Still, she had her suspicions, and when Pete had showed signs of depression not long after the marriage, she wasn't surprised.

Lew was six years younger than her brother and just three years old when their parents was killed in a car accident on an icy road. Their maternal grandfather, a kindly widower, had taken on the task of raising Lew and Pete the best he could. It had worked well. Pete loved science and the outdoors and became, first a science teacher, then a college professor, and finally president of the local community college. He had retired at fifty-five and became locally famous as an environmentalist and volunteer working to protect the loon population. Lew, on the other hand, had enjoyed working in her grandfather's sporting-goods store, which led to her love of fly-fishing. She had dropped out of college after her freshman year to get married, but after her divorce returned to earn a degree in law enforcement. Over the years, Lew and Pete had remained close. He had a daughter from his first marriage, Bridget, whom Lew loved as if she were her own.

"Have you called Bridget?" Was the first question Lew asked on arriving at the hospital. Linda was sitting with Pete's body in one of the critical-care rooms.

"I can't find her number," she said, raising teary eyes and waving one hand dismissively. That was Linda. Lew sighed. She turned and walked out of the room. Down the hall she spotted Ed Pecore, the Loon Lake coroner, in conversation with a young ER physician. As she walked up, she could smell him before she heard his voice. Pecore was saying, "Hell, Doc, you know it's a heart attack. That's what I'm putting down here on the old death certificate."

"I wouldn't do that," said the doctor. Looking over Pecore's shoulder, he saw Lew approaching and raised his eyebrows in her direction.

"Excuse me, Doctor, I'm Chief Ferris of the Loon Lake Police, but I'm also the sister of the individual back in that room. Pete Ferris is my brother."

"Dr. Gardner," said the young man, extending a hand to shake hers. "I was just telling this gentleman that for insurance purposes I recommend a pathologist examine the victim before we can establish cause of death. There's a serious contusion and scratches on the back of the neck that—"

"Oh, for Christ's sake, he fell and hit his head on a goddamn rock by the shore," said Pecore, interrupting. "Happens all the time."

"Ed," said Lew, struggling to keep her voice even as she spoke, "were you there when Pete fell?"

"No, but I see this all the time." Pecore's voice was ever so slightly slurred. "And she said so," he said pointing a finger at Linda, who had walked up while they were talking.

"Ed, for heaven's sake," said Lew. "What does Linda know? She's no health professional." Then turned to the ER doctor and said, "Thank you, Doctor. Let's keep my brother here in the hospital morgue and, following your recommendation, I'll file a formal request for an autopsy."

"That would be wise," said Dr. Gardner. "There is one difficulty, which is that the pathologist who conducts autopsies for St. Mary's Hospital is over in Green Bay and he's pretty backed up right now. You'd better plan for this to take two weeks or more. I'm afraid there's an expense involved, depending on insurance coverage . . ."

"No, Lewellyn," said Linda, stepping in front of Pecore. "I am not paying ten thousand dollars for an autopsy we don't need."

Lew stared at her. *Watch it*, Lew cautioned herself before adopting a no-nonsense tone to answer, "Don't worry, Linda, I'll pay for it. He's my brother and I would like to know when and how and why he died." She did her best to sound diplomatic, adding, "Who knows? Pete's death may have ramifications for my own health."

The ER doctor remained silent, watching both women.

Linda threw up her hands and stomped off, saying, "All right. Do what you wish. I'm going to get Pete's things from the nurse."

"Then you'll take care of the death certificate?" said Pecore, sounding uncertain. Lew knew that he was worried he would be caught making an error for the umpteenth time.

"I will. I'll work with the hospital and the pathologist's office to complete the paperwork. You don't have to be concerned with this. I'll handle it." She forced herself to say nothing more.

When Pecore was out of earshot, the ER doctor said, "That guy reeks of alcohol. How does he keep his job?"

"Married to the mayor's sister," said Lew. "Dr. Gardner, with my sister-in-law out of the way for a minute, please tell me what you think happened to my brother. Am I overreacting? Was it likely a heart attack?" She took a deep breath, forcing back tears.

"I'm not sure but I doubt it. On the other hand, I'm no pathologist," said the doctor. "But I don't like the bruising I see on the shoulders, the neck, the back of his head. Now he may have rolled down a rocky ledge that could cause that. I had a friend who was hiking the Grand Canyon and fell and—"

"Heavens," said Lew. "He was just over on Lynn Lake—a pond! That lake is no Grand Canyon. What confuses me is that Pete has been in excellent health and was only fifty-nine years old. I will definitely feel better if we have an autopsy." As she spoke, she tried to keep her voice from shaking, forcing herself to remain composed, even though her life as she knew it had just splintered.

"Frankly, I will, too," said the doctor.

Minutes later, standing outside by her cruiser, Lew hit the number on her cell phone for her niece and waited. The girl, a graduate student in Madison, answered immediately.

When she heard the news, Bridget was quiet for a long time. Her silence worried Lew. "Bridget, hon, would you like to come home and stay with me until we . . ." She couldn't bring herself to use the words "funeral" or "bury." She swallowed hard and waited.

"I'm okay," said Bridget, "but I need to tell you something. Dad was here last weekend and told me he was filing for divorce. Linda has been having an affair, but he hadn't been happy in that marriage anyway. Told me now he had an excuse."

"An affair?" Lew was surprised that she wasn't surprised. "With whom? Do we know the lucky guy? Sorry."

"Don't apologize, Aunt Lew. I feel the same way. No, he didn't mention a name and I didn't ask. I mean, it was so rarely that we had time together just the two of us that I didn't want to cloud the afternoon by saying much about that woman."

Again a long silence.

"Bridget? Are you going to be okay?"

"Not sure. But we had a really good time together, Dad and I . . ."

"Hold on to that, sweetheart. He would want you to remember him that way."

"I will. Every minute." A soft sob.

# Chapter Eight

~

After talking to Bridget, Lew got into her cruiser. Once inside, she hit a familiar number on her personal cell phone. The man who answered sounded so pleased at the sound of her voice that she hated to ruin his day.

"Sorry, Bruce, I'm not calling to invite you north to go fly-fishing, I'm afraid I have a very serious question"— before she could say more, she was sure she could see his happy, bushy eyebrows drooping—"I need to reach your new forensic pathologist. Would you happen to have his number handy?"

"*Her* number handy?" Bruce made sure she got the emphasis on his first word. Bruce was one of the best crime scene investigators with the Wausau Crime Lab— the "Wausau boys" as Lew referred to them whenever a homicide investigation required that she call on them for help. Since she'd taken over as chief, she had had to fight her way past the scorn of the crime lab director and his predecessor, who made their bias against women in law enforcement obvious by forcing her to jump through hoops of unnecessary paperwork when requesting assistance at a crime scene. Or listen to their inappropriate comments on the bodies or faces of the few females who dared to enter their field.

Not Bruce Peters. First, he was a good human being; second, he was a talented investigator who knew to look beyond the obvious; and third, he was desperate to improve his casting with a fly rod and knew Lew was the expert who could help him do so. Not only did they enjoy and respect each other, they enjoyed bartering their expertise—his for hers.

"Our new pathologist is Lisa Carter and I'll text you her number shortly. Mind if I ask why?"

"Not at all. And I may be overreacting, but my brother, who was just fifty-nine years old, has died unexpectedly. The ER doc who examined him this morning found bruising that he thinks merits an autopsy, at least to determine if it was accident or a health issue. Our coroner—you know old 'over-served' Ed—disagrees. He insists it must have been a heart attack—"

"Your *brother* died? Oh, my God, Chief. Are you okay?"

"Yes. At least I think so. Right now I just want to get an autopsy lined up."

"Say no more," said Bruce, "we know Ed. You can shoot a guy in the back of the head and he'll swear it's a suicide."

"Right," said Lew. "Just so you know, I'm planning to pay for this myself as I may be wrong but I just don't think . . ."

"Where did this happen?" Bruce's jovial tone had turned dark.

"Out on a small lake up here where he has been monitoring a loon nest. Two fishermen found him on the shore."

"How was he lying? On his back? Side? Facedown?"

"Don't know. I'm calling you first to line up the autopsy. Then I'm getting in touch with the two guys who found him. It's these bruises have me wondering what the hell happened."

"Has he had health issues?"

"No, and that's the thing. Pete's an outdoors guy, always has been, very active. Serious hiker, he runs. Hell, he spent a month this winter hiking New Zealand. Plus we're close. I would have known if he'd had heart issues, high blood pressure, whatever. He would have told me. But, again, I know I may be overreacting. Full disclosure, Bruce. I could have the pathologist who works with the hospital do the autopsy, but that has to happen over in Green Bay and they're backed up. I guess I feel like your people do a better job because they know enough to look for the unexpected. And maybe they aren't too busy?"

She was careful not to say too much. A cardinal rule is not to prejudice an investigator, much less a pathologist, with opinion or suspicion that might taint the analysis. No, she would make sure Bruce and his colleague knew that she was trying to save time and get a result she would have confidence in. That's not what she was feeling in her gut—but she had to keep her mouth shut.

"I owe you, Chief," said Bruce, "and I understand not wanting to wait on something so tragic. I'll put in for the autopsy with Dr. Carter. We had coffee just half an hour ago so I know she's got the time right now. Mind if I drive up with her? I'm curious about your brother's accident, if that's what it is, too. I spend plenty of time out on the stream by myself. Likely teach me to be more careful." She knew he knew what she was thinking. And he knew to keep his mouth shut.

Lew sighed with relief. Hanging up, she walked back into the hospital to the EMT office. The door was open, and she could see two men and a woman sitting around a small Formica-topped table drinking coffee and sharing a box of doughnuts while each was intent on the images on their cell phones. She knocked to get their attention.

At the sight of her one of the men jumped to his feet. "Chief Ferris, how are you?" It was Don Flatley, a veteran with the EMT crew whom she knew well. Lew explained that the victim they had just brought in was her brother.

"The ER doc told me that two fishermen found him and I need to talk to them," said Lew. "Do you have their names and how I can reach them?"

"Sure do. They were here until half an hour ago. They drove in right behind us, hoping your brother would be okay. Those guys are heroes the way they reached your brother and got him to us so fast. I've got cell numbers, but I'll bet they're out at Lynn Lake trailering their boat right now. They left it at the public landing."

Lew called the first of the two numbers that Don wrote down for her. No luck.

"If the guy has AT&T, he won't have service out there," said Don. "Try the other number."

Lew punched in the second number. On the fourth ring, she heard: "Stevens here. Who is this?"

Talking fast, Lew explained who she was and asked, "Are you at the lake right now, Mr. Stevens?"

"Yes, just hitching our trailer."

"Please, can you stay until I get there? I need you to show me where you found my brother."

"Not a problem, Chief Ferris. Tom and I feel so bad he didn't make it. Take your time—we'll be here."

*  *  *

Thirty minutes later, Lew was in the boat with Curt Stevens and Tom Gilley drifting toward the loon nest and the spot where they had found Pete.

"So this is where you climbed out of the boat and waded toward shore?" she asked Tom. Peering over the edge of the boat into the dark water dotted with weeds, she said, "Whoa, I can't thank you enough. I hope you're a swimmer."

Tom shrugged. "Fished this lake many times, Chief. I knew it had to be shallow. I'm a volunteer firefighter and I've had basic first-aid training, so I know how to check for a pulse, which is why I didn't hesitate. Knew we had to reach him fast. I was pretty surprised when I found he had a pulse. Curt threw me the life jackets and I was able to slip them under your brother's body so we didn't have to move him much to get him to shore over at the landing."

"And you never walked on shore here at this location? By the loon nest?"

"No." Tom gave her an odd look, "Should I have? I thought . . ."

"No, no, you did the right thing." She didn't add that approaching Pete from the water meant no one had trampled on the shoreline or the slight berm above the loon nest. The evidence of whatever it was that had caused her brother's fall should still be there.

"Excuse me while I make a quick call," said Lew, grabbing her cell and hitting a number in her key contacts.

"Sorry, Chief," said Ray Pradt. "I'm about to start my podcast. Call you in an hour—"

"No," said Lew, her voice shrill with anxiety. "No, I need you now. Right now." Tears pressed behind her eyelids, and the two fishermen in the boat looked at her with alarm.

Lew tried to calm herself, then said, "Sorry, Ray. I need to talk to you right this minute." She spilled out the story, explained where she was, and said, "if you can do that podcast later, then we have a chance to examine this area before any rain or animals or—"

"Got it," said Ray. "Be there in fifteen. The podcast is a mess anyway. I'll tackle it later. Need photos?"

"Might. Bruce Peters is on his way too. And, Ray, meet me at the end of Larson Road off old K. That's where Pete would park and walk in to check on his loons."

With the last two words, tears slipped down her cheeks. She tried to mumble a "sorry."

"He was your brother," said Tom Gilley, "don't apologize."

\* \* \*

Ray arrived to find Lew standing by her cruiser, which she had parked across the clearing from her brother's SUV. She waved at his battered blue pickup, motioning for him to park near her.

The morning was sunny, and the leaping musky that served as a hood ornament for Ray's truck shimmered in the bright light. She deliberately avoided looking at the word painted on the sign affixed to grill as a bug-catcher. Designed to be a humorous reference to the old pickup's owner, today it was not funny—*Gravedigger*.

"He would go in from here," said Lew, pointing to a narrow deer trail off the clearing that ran about fifty yards before dropping down toward the water. "You'll see the loon nest from the path when you get closer. Pete said they have two chicks right now."

"I know this area," said Ray. "Came here a lot as a kid. We called it Wolf Hollow. They probably still do." As he spoke, he reached behind the front seat of his truck for his camera bag.

It struck Lew that he was too quiet.

"Ray?" Lew waited but got no answer as he fumbled for his equipment. "What's wrong? I'm sorry, but I had to get you out here."

"My worry is . . . small potatoes," said Ray in his customary, halting delivery that drove people nuts. At least that was normal.

"What is it? Personal?"

"Kinda. I blew it on my podcast yesterday."

Lew relaxed. That *was* small potatoes but not, of course, to Ray, who had recently taken to boasting he had over half a million listeners tuning in to his fishing podcast: "listeners across . . . the . . . country."

"What happened?" Lew hoped the answer would come quickly. She wanted him to check Pete's movements through the brush as soon as possible.

"Oh, I named my best fishing spot and didn't realize it till later. Now every yahoo with a spinning rod will be out there . . . goddammit."

"Oh . . . you said the name of the lake and everything?"

"Yep."

She paused, remembering a class in public relations that she had taken when taking her law enforcement courses. "You know what a correction is when a newspaper makes a serious mistake in its reporting?"

"C'mon, Chief, I don't read the paper. I'm online, doncha know."

"Doesn't matter. All you do is this. When you start your podcast later today, first thing you announce is—and quote me: 'Correction necessary for yesterday's podcast. I specified the wrong lake, folks. You want the northwest bay on Lake George. That's where the big girls are.' That's all. Just leave it at that. Everyone won't get it, but it'll help redirect traffic."

"Yeah? You think there are fish there? Am I lying?"

"Ray, I have no idea, but let's keep busybodies out of your honey hole. They have fish locators, moon charts, astrologers—let 'em do their own research. Now, please, can you see if you can find any footprints here before they dry out in the sun?"

Ray's face had brightened. Before Lew could open her mouth to say more, he waved a hand to stop her. "I know what you want: can I find where he fell and why. Trust me, Chief, these eyes are working."

"Thank you. Now, I have to get back to the hospital. Bruce is driving up with their new pathologist and I need to meet with them." Even as she spoke, Ray was looking around the clearing. "Back out over there," he said, "I see where another car was in here this morning. Let's not mess up those tire tracks."

Getting into her cruiser, Lew felt a thud in her gut. Someone else had been there this morning? Who? Why? She knew that if anyone could answer those questions it would be Ray Pradt.

\* \* \*

Yes, Ray was a fine musky fisherman with a solid following on his podcast, but Lew knew he was unusual in another way. As a young boy, he had loved being in the forest and on the water. So much so that when he languished in school and his grades dipped, his parents despaired of him. After all, they had succeeded in raising one son who was an academic star and had become a hand surgeon and a daughter who also excelled in her studies and became a high-earning litigator in Chicago. What were these parents—Ray's father a physician, his mother a librarian—to do with a kid whose main achievement in life appeared to be catching bluegills?

And then there were his strange friends. Rather than hanging out with kids his own age, Ray loved listening to the stories told him by an old trapper, now in his nineties, who talked of the streams and lakes and how to scout for bigger fish: "Follow the signs left by the beaver and the eagles, the owls and the bobcats—them's the ones catch the trophies, boy." He tagged along after an elderly Ojibwa from the reservation who taught him how to read another set of signs: those left in the brush and the grass, the trees and the dirt; signs left by deer and bear, fisher and porcupine. Hunters all on land and water. No wonder Osborne's McDonald's buddies put up with Ray's bad jokes and challenging sentence structure: "He's got the eyes of an eagle, and that sonofabitch can track a snake over rock." Did his parents ever appreciate that? Not yet. "They keep hoping I'll grow up and make a living," he'd chuckle.

Lew knew Ray better. Yes, she had a file on his misdemeanors for buying and smoking pot, but that same file meant he could ask questions of bad actors who would never talk to her or her officers, bad actors who knew what really happened when bad things went down. He was her gateway to sources that had proved invaluable for saving lives. And that was worth more than "making a living."

# Chapter Nine

Back at the hospital, Lew tracked Dr. Gardner down in the ER and alerted him to the imminent arrival of the forensic pathologist from the Wausau Crime Lab. "She's new, so she may have questions about your operations here," warned Lew. Moments later Bruce Peters and Lisa Carter walked through the entrance to the Emergency Room.

*Oh, gosh, Dr. Lisa Carter doesn't look old enough to drive*, was Lew's first thought. Seconds later, humbled, she realized she herself was now old enough that anyone under the age of forty looked to her like a teenager.

Nearly six feet tall and rangy, the young pathologist struck Lew as an athlete, likely a runner or basketball player. She had a mop of short, naturally curly, light-brown hair, wide-open features, a generous smile, and lively, intelligent brown eyes. It was hard to imagine her spending her days indoors digging through dead bodies.

*But what do I know?* Lew asked herself with a shrug. *Whoever thought I'd grow up to carry a gun and chase bad guys? I was supposed to be a nurse or a schoolteacher.* She grinned to herself.

One thing was for certain: Dr. Lisa Carter carried herself in a way that inspired confidence. *"If this autopsy costs me ten thousand dollars,"* thought Lew, *"I already feel good about it."*

She caught Bruce watching her with a question in his eyes. When she gave him a nod of confidence, he relaxed. Lew handled the introductions, then sat down to wait while Dr. Gardner walked Bruce and Dr. Carter down to the hospital morgue.

Fifteen minutes later, they returned. Lisa Carter walked over to Lew and said, "Chief Ferris, you've made a wise decision. The bruises, the lacerations—"

"Lacerations?" Lew was surprised.

"Yes, the victim—I'm sorry, your brother—met with someone or something involving enough force that the skin is torn in several spots. If he fell, he could have been running from a threat—a bear? A wolf? I know there are bears in the woods up here, but I understand they rarely attack humans. And I'm new to Wausau from Kansas City so I'm not familiar with natural predators and their behavior patterns just yet."

"Wolves don't attack people either," said Lew. "Usually, unless . . ." She didn't finish her thought.

Dr. Carter shrugged. "Unless their prey is being threatened by another perceived predator. Bruce told me your brother was protecting a loon nest with young chicks. Correct?"

Lew nodded, stunned.

"During my residency in Colorado, I had the opportunity to examine victims of mountain lion attacks. I'll be able to tell if an animal predator was involved in your brother's death. Bruce told me you've requested my services," she said with a sympathetic smile, "so his body is being prepared for transport to my lab in Wausau. I can let you know within a few days what I learn."

"Thank you," said Lew, "I just . . . I need to know exactly what happened."

As they walked out of the hospital toward their vehicles, Lew said, "Bruce, just so you know—this is worth six weekends in the trout stream."

Overhearing her, Lisa looked at her colleague quizzically. "What does that mean?"

Bruce chortled and his eyebrows danced. "Chief Ferris moonlights as a fly-fishing instructor. She's been my teacher and my scourge for two summers now."

"I'm not stupid," said Lew with a wink at Lisa. "I know how to get the best of the Wausau boys on my cases."

"Wausau boys?" Lisa looked puzzled.

"That's what I call the guys from your Wausau Crime Lab. My predecessor, Chief Sloan, called 'em that, and it's stuck over the years. Say," said Lew, noticing they had stopped in front of two vehicles, "did you folks drive up in separate cars?"

"Yes," said Bruce, "I wasn't sure if I could talk you into taking a break for some time in the stream. My wife and daughter are visiting her family so I booked a room at the Loon Lake Inn overnight. But I understand if the timing is wrong. Got my gear and I'll head out on my own."

"Actually, I'm on my way out to the lake where they found my brother. Ray is there now. He was good enough to come right over."

Bruce looked over at Lisa, who was listening, and explained, "Ray Pradt is a local who often assists Chief Ferris on cases. He's an expert tracker and knows the water and woods around here better than anyone. An expert musky fisherman too, I might add."

"I'm liking this job more by the minute," said Lisa as she opened the rear door to her SUV to set her medical bag inside. "My dad was a big bass fisherman down in Missouri, so I grew up around spinning rods. Mind if I tag along? I'd like to meet this Ray guy and then I'll head back down to the office. Do you mind?"

"Follow me," said Lew, fairly certain that Ray Pradt was not going to mind meeting Dr. Lisa Carter.

\* \* \*

Ray was sitting in the cab of his pickup with the door open and his long legs braced on the running board. He was focused on reading something on his phone.

"Oh, hi, Chief. I'm just looking up where's the closest place to buy one of these." He held up a pry bar, and Lew was happy to see that he was wearing nitrile gloves. "Found it in the brush about fifty feet from where your brother went down."

While he was talking two more cars drove up—Bruce and Lisa Carter.

"It's Gearwrench, a type of pry bar they use for demolition, and these things ain't . . . cheap," he said stepping down from his truck. He nodded at Bruce and the newcomer. "Otherwise, disappointing news maybe 'cause there are so many footprints between this parking area and the spot right above the loon nest, it's hard to say who was here last. Hasn't rained in a week, which doesn't help either. I imagine that people with that Loon Rescue group check here a couple times a day, don't you think? It's like a parade of sightseers."

"I was afraid of that," said Lew. "Did you see where he fell?"

"Yes, and that's the odd thing. I can't see why he would have fallen. True, you have a slight slope down to the water but no roots or rocks to trip on. And he did hit hard. Almost as if he was pushed. I took photos of where he landed. But I do have very good news and . . ." Ray paused, as Lew knew he would.

She waited, Bruce waited, and Lisa looked puzzled.

"There are six trail cameras out there. Six! Let's go get the monitors. They should tell us everything we need to know. Speaking of which, who is this lovely lady? Oh, hi, Bruce."

Acknowledging he was of no interest whatsoever to the handsome fishing guide known to be addicted to ladies, Bruce shrugged and stepped aside so Ray could reach out to shake Lisa's hand.

Introducing Lisa, Lew said, "Dr. Carter has experience with victims of predators—"

"Mountain lions to be specific," said Lisa, stepping forward to give Ray's hand a hearty shake. "I'll be doing the autopsy, so if you don't mind, I'd like to see the location where this occurred."

"I'm . . . honored," said Ray with a bow and gestured toward the trail into the woods that overlooked the loon nest. "Follow me, everyone. Like I said, it's been a parade in here so you won't disturb anything along the trail."

Ten minutes later and back in the clearing, Ray held up the pry bar, which he had been holding onto. "So . . . this was thrown into the brush . . . like I said. Not dropped. I checked, and there was no sign of someone walking or running along there to have dropped it."

"May I see it?" asked Lisa. She had opened her car door and was pulling on nitrile gloves. Ray handed her the pry bar and she examined it carefully. "Yes, I'll need this," she said. Lew noted she was careful not to say more.

"Mr. Pradt," she said after storing the pry bar in an evidence bag that Lew had handed her, "very pleasant meeting you, and you, too, Chief Ferris. I'm going to head back to Wausau now." She climbed into her vehicle, gave a quick wave, and drove off.

The face Ray turned to Lew was serious. "Let's find those trail camera monitors."

"I know right where they are," said Lew. "Pete kept them in his garage. Follow me."

# Chapter Ten

Pete's house was less than twenty minutes from Lynn Lake. As Lew drove up to the garage, she checked for Linda's car, but she didn't appear to be home. She marched straight to the side door opening to the garage. Ray was at her heels, and Bruce pulled into the driveway just as she pushed the door open.

"Oops," she said at the sight of Linda's car. "I better let her . . ."

Too late. Linda dashed out of the front door, down the short walkway to the garage, and shouted, "What the hell are you doing, Lewellyn?"

Lew raised both hands in an attempt to quiet her down. "I am so sorry, but I didn't think you were here, Linda." She turned to the men. "You know Ray, and this is Bruce Peters with the Wausau Crime Lab. We're here to check the monitors for Pete's trail cameras."

"Fine," said Linda, spitting out the word. "Next time do me the courtesy of telling me you're coming.

Dammit." Turning, she flounced back to the front door, which she slammed shut behind her.

Lew gave a sheepish look as she motioned for Ray and Bruce to follow her in. "She's right, I should have called or knocked on the door."

"Such a pleasant person," said Ray as he followed Lew in.

They walked past Linda's vehicle and the empty space where Pete parked and through a doorway to a spacious workroom where Pete kept his bikes, a kayak, a canoe suspended overhead, golf clubs, and an assortment of backpacks, duffels, and four pairs of boots. In one corner, and set up on the wall so they could be watched from a well-worn padded office chair, were the monitors for four trail cameras.

"Pete showed me how to work these," said Lew as she flicked a switch on the wall. "It was right after my sister-in-law—his first wife—died, and he wanted someone besides himself to be familiar with the setup. I'm sure Linda has no idea how these work."

The images on the monitors sprung to life in full color as they showed what the cameras were capturing in real time. "Now, at night, the photos show up in black and white," said Lew.

"Of course," said Bruce, "I've seen plenty trail cameras. Let's replay last night."

"Right, but give me a minute. Pete said these will save two weeks of footage," said Lew as she checked the photo stream. "He set the motion detector to shoot every five seconds. He wanted the maximum so they could see patterns of activity in the woods and along the shoreline near the loon nest."

"The night is pretty quiet," said Bruce after a few minutes of nothing but owls showing up. "Let's check early morning . . . like before sunup."

"That's right where I'm going," said Lew. "We're all thinking the same thing." But the cameras, each focused on different angles, showed no unusual movement aside from the loons themselves shifting, resettling, and one swimming off.

"Where are the other two monitors?" asked Ray. "The cameras for those are rigged higher and farther back from the path that leads down to the shoreline. These are from cameras that are so low and close to the water that we're only getting views of movements awfully close to the nest. I'd like to see what's happening five, ten, fifteen feet back."

An unexpected knock at the doorway interrupted their concentration as a voice said, "Sorry, but the garage door was open and I heard voices. I just got the news about Pete. Are you Mrs. Ferris?" The woman stepped into the room with a quizzical glance at Lew's uniform.

Wearing black pants and a black sweater, the woman had a cap of short, straight gray hair and a brisk manner. Before she could ask another question, Lew stepped forward with her hand out, "I'm Pete's sister, Lewellyn Ferris." She gestured to her uniform. "A police officer."

"Oh," the woman said, "I'm Ann Mondale and I've been working with Pete on the Committee to Save the Pelican River. Today we were to meet with our lawyer and finalize the language on a lawsuit to stop the DNR from approving exploratory drilling. But now . . ."

She swallowed, trying not to sob. "Sorry." She looked at Lew. "Your brother was such a good man. What happened? Heart attack? A stroke? He seemed so young."

"Please come in," said Lew, welcoming her into the room. "That's what we're trying to figure out. Here's what happened," she said and gave a brief description of the fishermen finding Pete and explained why they were watching the monitors. "But we haven't seen anything unusual, so maybe it was his health."

The woman nodded. "I know he was dedicated to protecting the loons. That's how we met—through Loon Rescue. Oh," she choked again, "this is so . . . unexpected. He had so much energy." Her last word was lost in a sob.

"His wife is in the house if you want to say something to her," said Lew.

"Sure, I'll do that," said Ann, backing up. "I've never met her—do you mind telling me her name?"

"Linda," said Lew. "She may be a little . . . abrupt. She's pretty upset."

"Understandable," said Ann. With a gesture toward the monitors, she added, "Will you let me know what you find out?" Her expression turned shy. "I cared for your brother."

"Yes," said Lew. "Let me put your number in my phone."

After she was gone, Ray said, "Chief, we need to find the images from the other two cameras. Where do you think they might be?"

"I'll bet someone with Loon Rescue has them—maybe a couple people. I'll track down someone with the group and see if they can help us find them."

"That woman who was just here said that's how she met your brother. Maybe she knows," said Bruce.

Lew gave him a quick look and ran out into the garage. When she got to the door and checked the drive-way, the woman's car was gone. *Darn, but I have her cell number*, thought Lew.

She walked back into the workroom. "No luck. I'll try that cell number she gave me." Lew hit the number on her phone and listened to the ring. It cut off. "Shoot. I'll bet she's like the rest of us and gets so many robo calls that she doesn't answer strange numbers."

All three shrugged and looked frustrated. After exchanging cell-phone numbers, Bruce and Ray headed out of the garage.

\* \* \*

Lew walked over to knock on the front door before stepping in and calling Linda's name. Her sister-in-law strode into the foyer immediately with a scowl on her face.

"What?"

"Do you have Pete's keys? I'll get the car moved back into town and check it over before I return it."

"Check for what?" she said angrily as she thrust the keys at Lew. "Oh, never mind."

"One last thing," said Lew, forcing herself to remain civil. "Would you happen to have the name and number of anyone working with Pete at Loon Rescue?"

"No, I don't. That was Pete's way to waste time. I've had nothing to do with those people." She made it sound like anyone working to protect loons had to be a nutcase.

\*   \*   \*

Lew called Officer Adamczak, who was supposed to be on duty but was likely to be parked somewhere twiddling his thumbs. Lew was never surprised to find him sounding preoccupied and doing nothing.

Roger Adamczak had made a grave mistake several years earlier. When his small insurance firm had been struggling financially, he opted to enroll at the community college for law enforcement training. Lew was sure he thought life as a police officer in Loon Lake would be easy—parking tickets, maybe a drunk or two, and a nice retirement package. Piece of cake.

How wrong he was! Ever since he had joined the force there had been murders, kidnappings, drug busts—you name it. Life in these United States whether you live on a rural road or central city.

These days, while Roger Adamczak did not inspire great confidence in his colleagues should they find themselves in a life-threatening situation, they at least knew where to find him: sitting in his cruiser twiddling his thumbs or—as he liked to put it—"reflecting on life." This afternoon, he surprised Lew with his enthusiasm as he rushed to help her get Pete's car back to the station. She wanted it kept there until they had more information on cause of death. She also wanted to go through it in the hope he had left any notes or phone numbers of people who might have the missing camera monitors. A hurried look through the few papers on the old desk in his workroom had turned up nothing.

\* \* \*

Walking past the front desk at the police station she stopped for a hard, lingering hug from Marlaine, who was working Dispatch that afternoon. "I think Dani needs you," whispered Marlaine as she let go of her.

Lew nodded and headed down the hall to her IT assistant's cubicle.

"Chief," said Dani, glancing up from her computer, "I got more data on Noah McDonough. Do you have a minute?"

"I don't," said Lew. "Any chance it can wait until tomorrow morning? I'm exhausted."

"Of course," said Dani, "I'm so sorry about your brother. Oh, you do need to know that the judge's office called and pushed the McDonough arraignment up to tomorrow morning at nine AM. I hope that's okay"

Lew gave a weak smile. "Fine. I'll be in early tomorrow."

\* \* \*

Sitting on the sofa with Osborne that evening, Lew was unusually quiet. "Sorry," she had said to him earlier, "I'm not myself. Still recovering from the news." She curled closer to him.

"Don't be sorry. You've lost one of your dearest friends." Osborne wrapped his arms around her.

"I've lost my childhood."

He patted her shoulder.

The ten o'clock news came on and Lew was comforted that some things never change—the news always comes on.

"Breaking news today," said the news anchor, "Normandy Mining and Exploration announced late this afternoon that they have been granted a permit for exploratory drilling for potential sulfide mining on private land. The permit may encounter some pushback from a local activist group who insist the mining could endanger water quality along the Pelican River . . ."

"Hey," Lew sat up. "How much private land is there along the Pelican? I thought most of that was state forest and protected. Am I wrong?"

"I don't know," said Osborne. He jumped up and walked into his den, where he kept a county plat book. Bringing it back to Lew, who had straightened up on the sofa, the two of them paged through until they got to the map showing the properties along the Pelican.

Lew ran her finger across the page, then pointed and said, "The McDonough Family Trust is the only private owner along the river in this area. Has to be Grace McDonough who is letting them drill on her land. Now I know why I saw a Normandy Mining truck in her driveway."

"Must be," said Osborne. "If they find what they're looking for, she'll be worth even more money." He shook his head.

"And put the entire Pelican River at risk of contamination," said Lew. She leaned back against the sofa, her arms crossed and a grim look on her face.

"This may sound like a non sequitur," said Osborne, "but I took Mason fishing this afternoon." He winked at Lew, "I want her to know we still love her."

"See any fish?"

"No, but we were only out for an hour. She told me her pal, John, has been bragging that his dad is going to be making a lot of money—enough that he's going to let John buy a big fishing boat . . ."

"Ah, implying yours is small?"

"I guess so. Wonder what Stan is up do?"

"Maybe he's in on Grace's deal. He sure put up quite a defense of her in my meeting with the kids and their parents." Lew thought back over the meeting. "Now that I think about it, I badgered him a little, asking if she was a client, and he looked—for lack of a better word—guilty."

Lew's cell phone rang, and she looked down to see who could be calling so late and hoped it wasn't Dispatch with a call that would take her out into the night. "Oh," Lew was relieved to see the name on her screen. "It's that woman who was working with Pete on the mining issue. Excuse me, Doc. I need to take this."

As she answered the phone, she got to her feet. "Yes, this is Chief Ferris. What is it, Ann?"

"Sorry to call so late, Chief Ferris, but I was able to locate who has the feed for those two trail cameras. Diane Fennema is her name. She has the images sent to her phone so she can check it anywhere."

Ann gave a soft chuckle and added: "She's a lot younger than me and much more high tech, so I don't know how she does that. But the frustrating news is that she's camping this week up on Isle Royale and has her phone turned off."

"What? Why would she do that?" Lew was flummoxed. For one thing, the weather was still pretty cool for camping, and for another—why turn your phone off?

"She's a wildlife specialist doing research on wolf populations. When she's working in the field like she is this week, she can only be reached in an emergency."

"This is an emergency," said Lew.

"I knew you would say that, so I've got her number, and I'm sure you can leave a voicemail that will alert her to your situation, Chief Ferris. I've left one already myself so she has some idea why you might be calling."

"Thank you, Ann, I'll leave her a voicemail right away."

"Something else we didn't discuss and I think you should know, Chief. Last week when your brother and I were putting together the plan to push back against the proposed sulfide mine project, he told me he'd received an anonymous letter warning him not to interfere. Whoever it was knew that he checked on the loon nest because they left the letter under his windshield wiper when he was parked out at Lynn Lake doing it.  Now, on that day he had taken a group of Loon Rescue volunteers in to see where the nest was located, so it could have been someone in that group, but I doubt it. People who want to protect loons aren't in favor of polluting rivers. At least I'd be surprised."

"So someone could have been stalking Pete?"

"That's a tough way to put it," said Ann.

\* \* \*

Lew left a voicemail for Diane Fennema, then sank back down on the sofa. "How much money do you think Grace could get for that land, Doc?"

"If they find the traces of copper, nickel, and the other minerals they want, I imagine we're talking millions. Several million at the very least, but likely more. Depends."

Osborne could see Lew's mind working. "Hey," he said, "You need a good night's sleep. Forget everything for five minutes and let's walk down to the dock and say goodnight to the moon—guarantees a good night's sleep."

Lew pulled the jacket he offered around her shoulders and followed him down the stone stairway to his dock. As they stood together facing the moonlit lake, a steady breeze blew toward them.

Though Osborne had wrapped his arms around her, Lew felt alone. She gazed out across the dark, silent lake and found no answer for her grief.

# Chapter Eleven

❧

It was six fifteen in the morning that Thursday when Lew placed her first call to Diane Fennema. She got voicemail. At six thirty she tried again. Voicemail.

"I think I'll go nuts if I don't reach her soon," said Lew, when she caught Osborne watching her the third time she tried the number.

"Want me to drive up there?" Osborne said. "It's only a day trip . . . maybe."

They both knew that getting to Isle Royale up on Lake Superior depended on weather plus other factors.

"I'm sure I'll reach her today," said Lew. She closed her eyes, clenched her teeth, and said, "I just need to be patient."

Osborne gave her a sympathetic smile as he handed her the usual travel mug of hot coffee.

\* \* \*

On arriving at her office, she tried again. No answer. Dani poked her head in and asked: "Is this a good time to give you an update on what I learned about Noah McDonough? You have the bond hearing at nine, so it might be helpful . . ."

"Yes, please, come in," said Lew, pushing her chair back.

"Pretty simple," said Dani. "He's been accused but not convicted in three different incidents involving young girls. I guess since he wasn't convicted that it could be argued he doesn't have to register as a sex offender but—"

"A big *but*," said Lew. "I wonder how much his mother's money has played a role in all that? She can certainly afford the best legal muscle."

Dani nodded glumly. "Awful how some people can pay their way out of criminal behavior."

Lew smiled as she said with a chuckle: "Dani, don't even get me started. Say, on another matter, I've learned that this woman who was helping my brother with Loon Rescue may have the video from two trail cameras on her cell phone. Is that something I can ask her to e-mail to us?"

"Sure. Shouldn't be a problem, Chief. Here's my number so you don't have to look for it on your phone. Oh, hey, it's ten to nine. I think you need to be in court."

Lew made another call to Diane Fennema's cell. Still no luck.

The courtroom was ready: the judge, the court reporter, Lew, and Grace's lawyer. They waited. No sign of Grace and Noah.

At twenty after nine, Lew left the courtroom for a minute and tried Diane Fennema again. No luck. She went back into the courtroom.

Everyone was waiting, and Lew could see the judge fidgeting. She didn't blame him. This was rude and likely typical of Grace McDonough, who assumed the world turned around her busy, important life. Her lawyer kept making calls from where he was, also fidgeting.

At ten o'clock they gave up. "Maybe, your Honor," said her lawyer, "she got the time wrong." At that moment, Lew saw a call from Diane Fennema on her phone and ran out of the room.

"I am so sorry, Chief Ferris," said a woman's voice between crackles on the line, "and my connection up here is bad, so if I lose you I'll call right back. Ann told me about your brother Pete, and I am devastated. He was so nice and did so much for our loon rescue efforts—and education. He gave talks around the region for us. Anything I can do—please tell me."

"Ann said you might have several of the trail cameras streaming on your phone?"

"Yes, though I've been working our wolf project so I haven't checked them in a couple days. I will now."

"That would be good," said Lew, "but even better if you can send it to the number I'm going to give you, which is my IT expert here at the Loon Lake police station. We'll be able to see everything on her computer screen. I hope to find out exactly what happened to Pete. Did he collapse from a heart attack or . . . who knows?"

She didn't finish her sentence. She didn't want to sound like a nutcase for saying "I know my brother didn't die that way." She had no reason to believe that, she knew, except for the feeling in her gut.

But Diane didn't need an excuse. "I'll send it immediately," she said. "One thing I'd like to point out is that I encouraged Pete to set two trail cameras up higher and back about ten yards from the other cameras, as there is a wolf pack in that area. With the full moon due two nights ago, I wanted to be sure we didn't have wolves stalking beaver or raccoons and driving them down toward the loon nest. I thought we might have a better chance of spotting any predators under the light from a full moon, assuming no cloud cover, that is. So if you see what appears to be wolves or wolf cubs, please let Ann know ASAP, as the Loon Rescue folks will want to take steps to protect the loons."

"I didn't know wolves were a problem there," said Lew.

"They may not be, but my job with Loon Rescue has been to be sure they aren't. When you get the feed from the cameras, you need to know that I have each trail camera on a sensor that will snap pictures every five seconds when motion is detected. I know that's different from how Pete set the other cameras. So no movement, no image. And Chief Ferris, if you're going to be looking at the feed within the hour, I will have my phone on. Please call if there is a problem. More important, though, I am *so* sorry to hear what has happened. Your brother was a special person in my world."

"Thank you," said Lew, her voice soft. "Thank you."

*   *   *

Ten minutes later, the feed came through to Dani's computer. Lew had pulled her chair close to the screen alongside the young woman, and the two of them leaned forward and watched the images flash by. It didn't take long for Dani to find the feed for the night that Pete had last walked down the path to check on the loon nest.

"Owl," said Dani under her breath at the first black-and-white image. The next photo showed the back of a man wearing a loose-fitting pullover and a baseball cap. Several images in a row indicated that he was moving away from the camera.

"That's Pete," said Lew. "I'd recognize his stoop and that hat anywhere. This is great—oh, wait . . ." The final image showed the man's figure lower than the camera.

"Does the path slope downward?" asked Dani.

"Yes." Lew held her breath as another image flashed. It showed the back of a person in a windbreaker and tall enough that the head was hidden by branches. The figure held an object in its right hand but it was half obscured by the shape of the body. Again the figure, like the first one of Pete, dipped in a final shot and disappeared.

The next image showed the figure back in camera range but with its head down so the face couldn't be seen. "Windbreaker, no hat," said Dani, her voice tense.

"Different person," said Lew. "Does the camera record the time when these images were captured?"

"Yes." Dani checked and said, "Looks like your brother went down the path five minutes before the second person. Then it's a good ten minutes before we see the figure in the windbreaker back up on the path.

"What do you think he's carrying?" Lew held her breath.

"Not sure. A stick of some kind? Maybe they were using a cane?"

They continued to watch images flash by, but only owls and two deer showed up.

"Can you enlarge the images with the second figure?" asked Lew.

"I'll try," said Dani, "but not sure we can get much more than what we see here. I know you'd like to be able to see a face, but I don't think that's possible."

Lew sat thinking. "I'll call Ann and see if she can check with the Loon Rescue people and find out if anyone else was working with Pete that night."

"Wouldn't she have told you that?" asked Dani.

"You'd be surprised what people don't think about until you ask," Lew replied, keeping her tone level even as, for the first time, she felt a surge of hope.

*   *   *

By four o'clock that afternoon, Lew hadn't heard anything from the judge's office about Grace and Noah having been reached and the bond hearing rescheduled. She looked at her watch, then at the stack of paperwork, and decided to take her chances and leave early.

"My place tonight," she said to Osborne from her cell phone as she packed up to leave the office, "does a shrimp pasta sound good?"

"Are you sure, Lewellyn?" he asked. "It's only been a day since Pete . . . well, you can't be feeling that good. Let's do one more night at my place. Plus I've got a couple of inside tips for you," he teased.

"What?"

"Nope, you have to hear it here." She smiled for the first time that day as she ended the call. Walking past the front desk, the young woman on Dispatch waved for her to stop.

"Sorry, Chief, but I'm having a hard time hearing some old guy who's trying to call in an accident, something about a car and a river somewhere. I keep dropping him before I can hear more."

Lew set down her briefcase and hurried back to Dani's office. "Can you help Kristine on Dispatch? She doesn't seem to be able to get a good connection with an emergency call."

Dani followed Lew out to the front desk, where she guided the woman on Dispatch, who was new to the position, on how to run a GPS trace to locate the general area from which the call was coming.

Lew stood aside watching the two women, thankful again that she had enticed Dani away from the community college where she had been majoring in cosmetics and hair design. Though Dani still dressed like a twenty-three-year-old hairdresser, with long, artfully curled brown locks and skillfully applied eyeliner and mascara (plus artful eyebrows that Lew noticed changed from week to week), she couldn't mask her natural talent for IT.

Within seconds, Dani had the location: "Chief Ferris, he's just past the Thunder Bay Bar on a forest service road running along the Spider River."

"I know right where that is," said Lew. "Does it sound serious or just somebody stuck in a ditch?"

Kristine answered. "I keep hearing 'car' and the word 'bridge' come through. Is there a bridge out there?"

"Yes," said Lew, "there's an old bridge where the road runs alongside an abandoned railroad trestle. Should've been condemned years ago and the county has tried to block it off but some locals still use it. Oh, gosh, I hope no one has drowned. I keep telling the county they should tear the damn thing down. I'm on my way. Tell the old man someone will be there in ten to fifteen minutes."

As she drove, she alerted Officer Todd Donovan, who was on duty that afternoon. The two of them arrived at the old bridge at same time. A red Ford F-150 pickup was parked to one side of the road, and its driver, an elderly man in Carhartt overalls and a Milwaukee Brewers baseball cap, waved them down.

"I live down the road there," he pointed, "and I keep an eye on this bridge'cause it's gonna go one of these days. But look over there—that's new. Saw the damage to the railing last night. Guess I should've called then. Sorry."

A gaping hole could be seen on one side of the wooden bridge, which had been built in the early 1900s for use by loggers. Two of the wood railings designed to protect trucks using the bridge were missing.

"See what I see?" asked the old man, leaning over the edge of the bridge as he pointed down toward the water.

Though the river water was dark with tannin, the late afternoon sun penetrated far enough that Lew could see what appeared to be the top of a dark-colored vehicle. She hit the number on her cell phone for the towing service the department used for illegally parked cars and accidents.

When the owner answered, she gave directions to the location and said, "Tell your driver to bring a wet suit.

He'll have to wade into the river to hook this up, I'm afraid."

She listened to a question from the towing service owner, then looked over at the old man. "How deep is it here? Any idea?"

"Ten feet," said the old man, "we used to dive off this bridge when we were kids."

"Guess he won't be wading," Lew told the owner.

\*     \*     \*

Forty-five minutes later, the tow-truck operator surfaced after getting the vehicle hooked up and ready to be dragged from the river. "The driver is in there," he said the third time he surfaced. Still wearing his wet suit, he started the tow truck and moved forward slowly, slowly, until the top of the vehicle broke the surface of the Spider River—a black Range Rover.

He pulled farther ahead until the entire car was out of the water.

"Hold on, I'll check the interior," said Lew as the tow-truck operator jumped from his truck and started toward the Range Rover. She peered through the window on the driver's side.

No wonder Grace McDonough hadn't appeared for the bond hearing.

# Chapter Twelve

Lew tried Bruce's cell phone twice before he answered. "What's up, Chief? I'm out on the boat with Ray trying for a big girl on my fly rod."

"Sorry to ruin your day but we got work to do," said Lew. She gave him a brief description of what she was looking at and directions.

After checking her watch before making the next call, she knew what she was about to hear. With a grim smile she punched in the number for the Loon Lake coroner's cell phone.

The slurred "hello" was all she needed.

"Never mind," she said to Pecore. She hung up and without hesitation called Osborne. "Doc . . ."

"Lewellyn, don't tell me you'll be early for dinner—that's a first."

"Sorry, Doc. Afraid I have to deputize you again as Loon Lake's acting coroner." After explaining what was happening at the bridge, she said, "I tried Pecore knowing his 'happy hour' launched two hours ago, so you know the drill."

He did, and he was at the bridge in less than thirty minutes. Bruce was right behind him.

Osborne's certification that Grace McDonough was no longer alive took less than three minutes. After a perfunctory examination of the corpse, he approved the removal of the body from the Range Rover by the EMT crew, which had arrived shortly after him.

Sitting in the front seat of his Subaru with the door open while Lew and Bruce stood nearby, he filled in a few lines on the death certificate, then said, "I am not stating 'cause of death'—I'll leave that for Bruce's colleague, the new pathologist."

"Could it be suicide? Or maybe she was drunk," said Bruce.

"Drunk doesn't make sense as this is so far from her home, but on the other hand we aren't far from Thunder Bay Bar," said Lew. She didn't say what she suspected the three of them were thinking—suicide not likely. Drunk maybe. Grace could be one of those for whom drinking was a favorite sport.

"Already called Dr. Carter," said Bruce. "She's arranging for the body to be sent down to our morgue tonight. And, Chief Ferris, with your approval, I'd like to have the Range Rover parked in your police department garage. Until we know cause of death, I'm going to be careful. The EMT crew has been great about not touching any surface they didn't have to."

"Good," said Lew. "I've got Officer Donovan driving out to the family home to let her son know what's happened." She glanced at her watch before adding, "Hold on, he left here almost an hour ago. I wonder why he hasn't called."

"Todd," she asked after reaching the officer on his cell phone, "have you spoken with Noah McDonough?"

"He's not here, Chief," said Todd. "The front door was unlocked, so I called in loudly but no answer. I've knocked on windows, the back entrance, and looked all around. No one's here. I see a Toyota SUV parked in the garage but, again, no one's around."

"Strange," said Lew. "Stay out there another hour, Todd. If he's not back by then, I'll have Roger relieve you. The kid could be hanging out with friends somewhere and we've got his phone so we can't call him. Unless . . ." She didn't finish what she was thinking—that Noah could have a new prepaid phone they couldn't trace.

The more she thought about that, she remembered how curt he had been with his mother. Could Grace be more of a disciplinarian that it had appeared and her son was furious? There was evidence he wasn't normal in his behavior when it came to young girls. What about women? Like his mother?

Maybe she should be putting out an APB on Noah McDonough. On the other hand, he could be with friends and likely to be grief-stricken when he heard the news about his mom. Lew decided to wait until she knew what the situation was.

When the ambulance had driven off and the tow truck driver given instructions on where to park the Range Rover, Lew thanked the elderly man for calling in what he "should assume is an accident." After checking her watch, she turned to Osborne and Bruce. It was past eight o'clock. "Looks like pizza at the Loon Lake Pub, people."

"Sounds good to me," said Bruce. Osborne nodded in agreement.

"I wonder if the two of you would mind if after we get a bite to eat we stop by my office. I'd like to show you the images from the trail camera that this woman who's with Loon Rescue sent me earlier. They appear to show a person going down the path to the loon nest right after Pete the morning he died. I was going to ask you to view it with me tomorrow, but with all this happening, I'd feel better if we did it tonight."

An hour later the three of them gathered around Dani's computer as Lew pulled up the file with the images from the two trail cameras that had been placed farther back and higher than the four cameras they had already reviewed. They watched in silence as the images appeared, one after the other, on the screen.

"I'm surprised how clear these are," said Bruce. "Are those cameras equipped with floodlights?"

"No, it was a full moon that night. Diane Fennema is the woman who set up the trail cameras. She's a wildlife expert with the state, and she's been researching the stalking patterns of beavers and raccoons as well as fox—the larger predators known to attack loons. She and Pete positioned the two cameras to watch the path closer to the deer trail, which larger animals use."

After going twice through the photos that followed those of Pete going down the path, Bruce turned to Lew, his eyebrows furrowed and worry in his voice as he said: "Definitely another person there that night. You got a predator all right— a wolf, a human wolf."

"That's exactly what I think. Question is who could that be? Were they still there when Pete fell? If he fell?"

"Plenty of questions," said Osborne. "You need Ray to take a look at these. He knows what to look at beside the obvious."

"You're right," said Lew. "Now if I can tear him away from his stupid podcast . . ."

"Hold on, Chief," said Bruce, "his podcasts are pretty darn good. He's working on one right now with a guy who builds bamboo fly rods, so be kind. Okay?"

"I'll try." Lew gave a grudging smile.

\*   \*   \*

That evening as they settled in to sleep, Lew poked Osborne in the shoulder. "Hey, I almost forgot. You said you had a tip for me. What is it?"

"May not be a surprise tip after all," said Osborne, "but having coffee this morning, Art Higgins said he stopped in at the Pine Bar the other night after fishing and saw Grace McDonough there with Stan Mayer. He said they were pretty soused and the bartender hoped they weren't planning to drive themselves home. He had already called a taxi for them."

"We have only one taxi in Loon Lake," said Lew.

"Right. Art said the bartender said that the taxi guy wasn't surprised to get the call saying, 'those two—again?' So maybe Grace does have a drinking problem,"

"You'd have to if you're gonna hang out with Stan Mayer," said Lew.

"So you've got a drunken summer romance with an unhappy ending," said Doc.

"Wouldn't surprise me," said Lew as she turned over and tried to fall asleep. She was almost there when her cell phone rang.

"Chief Ferris?" the female voice sounded familiar, but Lew couldn't place it at first. She struggled to sit up in bed as she said, "Yes, who is this?"

"Oh, I'm sorry. Lisa Carter—Bruce said it would be okay to call you this late. Hope you don't mind. I just got the lab results on your brother's autopsy and another analysis I had done."

Wide awake in an instant, Lew sat up. "Sure, Dr. Carter, this is fine."

"First, he did not have a heart attack or a stroke, Chief Ferris. Your brother died of blunt-force trauma—two blows: one to the back of his head, one across his neck and shoulders."

Lew was silent for a beat then whispered, "I knew it."

A curious sensation swept through her: satisfaction mixed with anger and determination.

"You'll remember I insisted on taking that pry bar that the fishing guy found?" Lisa continued. "I saw some stains on it that I wanted to check out. They're bloodstains."

"But I didn't see any blood on Pete's body."

"A contusion and scrape across the back of his shoulders. The blood from that likely got rubbed off when the ER nurses removed his clothing. If possible, could you get that shirt from his wife? I hope she hasn't washed it."

"First thing in the morning," said Lew.

"My analysis shows the blood on the pry bar is a match with your brother's blood."

After the call, Lew shared the news with Osborne, who put his arms around her as she lay thinking hard. After a few minutes, she got up and reached for her cell phone to place a call.

"Roger?" she asked her officer assigned to watch the McDonough home. He sounded so drowsy she wondered if he had indeed fallen asleep on the job.

"Chief—yeah, no sign of the guy."

"No car pulled in? Nothing?"

"No, I'm here in the driveway. I would've seen."

"Okay, thanks, Roger. I'll call the sheriff's office and put out an APB. If he hasn't shown up by one AM, you can go home."

# Chapter Thirteen

It was her first cup of coffee of the day, she was still in bed, and Lew had to sit on her hands to resist calling Osborne's neighbor. After all, it was five thirty on a Saturday morning. *Be kind*, she told herself.

Osborne saw the impatience on her face. "You have to wait until six."

"You know me too well," she said with a laugh. "But you're right."

Two seconds before six, they heard a familiar knock on the window over the sink and looked up from the kitchen table where Osborne had just set down a plate of scrambled eggs dotted with bits of Neuski bacon. Without waiting for anyone to open the back door, Ray was in the kitchen, coffee mug in hand.

"Hey, Chief, I have a new idea for my podcast—"

"Ray, I need you to go right back to Lynn Lake. Got the call late last night: Pete was murdered."

Ray's mouth dropped open. He set his mug of hot coffee down on the counter, folded his arms, and leaned back. "Whoa. What? Why? I know you thought I rushed checking the path down to the loon nest but I was careful. I—"

"Dr. Carter, the new pathologist working with the Wausau boys, called me to report the autopsy showed blunt-force trauma."

"Oh." Ray was quiet. "The pry bar."

"Yes. The pry bar. The stains on it were blood, and they match Pete's. I know you checked close around the path that Pete took. But before you go back out there, I want you to see the new trail camera footage that I got yesterday. It shows someone walking down the path to the loon nest shortly after Pete."

"I told you so many people walk that area—"

"I know, I know. I'm not saying you missed anything. And who knows, once you see the images from the cameras you may recognize the person. I don't. All you can see is their back. What's significant is the timing recorded by the cameras, which is within minutes of Pete passing by and so early in the morning that I doubt it's someone from Loon Rescue."

"Okay, I'll head into town right now," said Ray, picking up his mug. "I'll cancel a guiding client I have this morning and go back to the lake. But this time I'll walk a wider perimeter in case I missed something."

"We're all human," said Lew. She didn't add that she recalled how frustrated he'd been with his podcast that morning; he could have been less than focused. "And Ray, we'll discuss that new idea for your podcast later today. Okay?"

He walked away, his right hand raised with the index finger pointing up as he answered, "Later is good."

Lew could tell he felt bad. If there is anything new to be found, he would make sure to find it.

\* \* \*

Half an hour later, sitting with Lew as Dani pulled up the images that Diane Fennema had sent from the two trail cameras that had been set higher, Ray studied each shot. He had Dani go back and forth several times, rewatching the frames from the images of Pete walking down the path to those of the individual following him moments later. Then the images—and timing—of that person who appeared to be hurrying back up the path with their face hidden by branches.

"The only detail that stands out to me," said Ray, thinking out loud, "is how they walk, maybe that jacket they're wearing. The images are not real clear, which is true of trail cameras, but the hunched shoulders help." He pushed his chair back from the computer monitor. "Thanks, Chief, I'm outta here. Call you when I'm finished."

"Where's he going?" asked Dani after he'd left. She'd been standing to one side so Ray could have her chair.

"Back to Lynn Lake. He's going to check the path and all around the area once more."

"He found the pry bar. You think there's more?"

"I think he has a better idea what to look for. By the way, thank you for coming in on a Saturday."

Dani grinned as she said, "No problem so long as it doesn't interfere with my hair appointment."

* * *

Back at her desk, Lew checked in with the sheriff's office, but no sign of Noah. "We're on it," said deputy who answered her call. "Got cars across the county keeping an eye out."

"He could be hiding," said Lew. "I have reason to believe he may be involved with his mother's death."

"Jeez," said the deputy. "I'll be sure everyone knows to watch for any sign of off-road travel, too. Is he dangerous? Armed?"

"No idea. Please tell people to be careful."

The minute she got off the phone, Lew questioned her assumption about Noah. After all, she had no proof, except it was suspicious he was gone. He should have been at the bond hearing with his mother, and now, a day later, he was still gone. So where the heck was he? Could he be driving back to Palm Springs? Maybe she should extend the APB beyond the Wisconsin borders.

The phone rang again, "Chief Ferris?"

"Good morning, Erin. If this is about the campaign, I'm sorry but I've got too much happening to even think about it."

"No, I'm calling because Mason told me something at breakfast this morning I think you should know. She said her friend, John—you know John Mayer, Stan's son—confided he's upset that his dad has a new girl-friend, and he hates her but he thinks his dad might marry her."

Lew gave an inner sigh of exasperation but knew she'd better listen. *Sheesh. Kids.*

"It's Linda," said Erin.

"Linda who?"

"Your sister-in-law. John told Mason his dad's been meeting her out at the family cottage for the last couple months. John knows because he sees the texts on his dad's iPhone when he sneaks it to play video games. I'm sure Stan has no idea the kid is on his phone. When I asked my daughter how John manages to use his dad's phone so much, he told her his dad stays out late, goes right to bed when he comes home—and leaves his phone charging on the kitchen counter. I thought you'd want to know 'cause Dad just called to tell me that Pete may have been murdered. I don't want to make you feel worse than you do already but . . ."

"No, gosh no, Erin. Thank you for telling me."

Before her phone could ring again, Lew called Lisa Carter. "Dr. Carter, any news of how Grace McDonough may have ended up in the river?"

"Sorry, Chief, afraid I'm still running tests, but I am estimating the time of death was twenty-four hours before the body was pulled from the river. Afraid I have to do more testing before I can say more. The cold water in the river had an effect on rigor mortis, as did the fact the woman was heavy. But I can say without question that the victim was dead before the car went into the river."

"Thank you, Dr. Carter. We still have no sign of her son, so he has just become 'a person of interest.'"

"Um," said Lisa. "I have an unrelated question if you don't mind."

"Please," said Lew, "anything I can help with?"

Lisa Carter chuckled. "Not sure. After we all met yesterday, it occurred to me that someone in the group—you, perhaps, or that guy who found the pry bar—Bruce told me the two of you do a lot of fishing?"

"I fly-fish," said Lew. "My colleague, Ray Pradt, he's a musky and walleye guy and fishes with a spinning rod. Are you familiar with any of this?"

"Not really, but I inherited a fishing pole, and I'd appreciate if someone could take a look at it and tell me what I have. My grandfather left it to me. My parents were divorced when I was young and I spent a couple summers with my dad. Dad and I would go fishing with my grandfather. I had a cane pole and a worm—I was maybe eight years old—but I had a good time and Grandpa knew it."

"One of us can help you, I'm sure," said Lew. "And if you're at all interested in fishing, you've moved to the right place."

"Well, I might be. I'd like to know more. Maybe I should hire that guide Bruce keeps telling me about."

"You mean Ray?"

"I think so."

Lew smiled to herself. She'd been wondering how long an attractive single woman could resist the six foot four, lanky, good-looking, and winsome Ray. She'd already noticed Lisa was not wearing a wedding ring.

"I'll tell you what, Dr. Carter," said Lew, "we have a motto up here: when it comes to fishing if you don't have time, you make time."

Again, she heard the chuckle.

"So what are you doing this afternoon?"

"Really? You're not kidding me?"

"If you're up for an initiation to fly-fishing." Lew didn't add her own personal take on the motto: when she needed time to think, it was time to be in the trout stream.

# Chapter Fourteen

～

Knowing Bruce would be heartbroken if he learned she had waded into the Prairie River without him, Lew hit his number on her cell phone.

"You're kidding!" said Bruce on the phone, with so much enthusiasm that Lew could hear his eyebrows levitate. "Can't believe this is working out after all."

"Ninety minutes in the parking lot here at the station," said Lew. "I'll head out to my place right now, get Nellie, and be back by then. Do you mind if Dr. Carter drives with you? You know Nellie—not much room in my old crate."

"Deal."

Next she called her best friend, who would also be heartbroken if he wasn't included. Osborne's phone buzzed against his hip where he had stashed it in his back pocket.

"Doc?" asked Lew in a light-hearted tone he hadn't heard in days. "What are you doing? Got time to join me and Bruce and our new pathologist out on the river?"

"Music to my ears, sweetheart," said Osborne, who had just been thinking that if she was planning to work another long day, he'd put Mike in the boat and go check out his secret musky waters—the two he kept secret even from Ray. This sounded more fun.

"Good. After what's happened this week, I need a break."

Lew gave him the details and hung up feeling downright buoyant. She was about to spend her afternoon with three people who were neither criminals nor dead. For one second, the campaign snuck into her thoughts. She knew Erin would prefer that she spend the afternoon knocking on doors. Nope. Not doing it.

Another thought she had as she drove home to pack up Nellie, her trusty, rusty pickup that she used exclusively for fishing, was that Pete would be with her in spirit. He had loved fly-fishing, though not as obsessively as his little sister. Lew smiled to herself as she drove; she had a sense she would feel Pete's spirit the moment she stepped into the river.

As she drove up the dirt lane leading to her little farmhouse, for the first time since the call about the kids attempting their citizen's arrest, she paid attention to the loveliness bursting everywhere: the bright-green needles on the tamarack, the spritely boughs of balsam and pine no longer burdened with snow, the budding leaves on the birch and maple, the oaks and the tag alder; even the crocus and trillium hiding under the old hemlock had awakened. And she had almost missed it!

After slipping her fly rod and gear into the bed of the pickup and as she was pulling on her fly-fishing vest, she had one last thought. She ran back into the house to grab her daughter's waders in case the good doctor had none, which was more than likely.

\* \* \*

At the clearing where she liked to enter the river, Lew pulled up and was climbing out of her truck when two familiar SUVs pulled in to park alongside Nellie.

It was an early May afternoon, the sun high and the water sparkling as it swirled around the rocks and through the riffles. Lisa Carter jumped out of Bruce's SUV wearing hiking shorts, a long-sleeved T-shirt, running shoes, and a baseball hat. While Lew and Doc were pulling on their waders, Lisa walked over to them. Lew looked up and started to say, "Dr. Carter—"

"Lisa, please," said the younger woman, correcting her.

"Okay, Lisa." Lew smiled. "Do you have waders?"

"Um . . . no. Didn't think I needed any yet."

"Thought so," said Lew as she threw a canvas bag at her. "What size shoe do you wear?"

"Eight and a half."

"Good. Those are my daughter's waders and her boots. She lives in Milwaukee and uses them when she visits with my grandchildren. They should fit you okay. Her foot's a little larger."

Lisa dumped the waders and boots onto the ground and studied the heap. "Mind if I ask how these work exactly?"

"Pull the waders on. You'll see they have feet on them; the boots go on over those. There should be a belt in there too, which you wear outside the waders."

Bruce, meanwhile, was busy pulling on his waders while Lisa got hers on pretty fast. After adjusting the straps and clinching the narrow belt around her waist, she walked over to Bruce's SUV and reached inside. She pulled out a long narrow case with a rusted, dented cap on it.

"Want me to use this fishing pole?" asked Lisa as she tried to unscrew the top. It wouldn't budge.

"First, it's not a pole," said Lew. "That's probably a fly rod. Not to hurt your feelings but, please, never call it a 'pole.'"

"Oh, gosh," said Lisa, laughing. "Now you know I'm a beginner."

Bruce, who had joined in the laughter while he assembled his own fly rod, set it aside and reached over to help Lisa.

"No, no, don't take that out of the case," said Lew. "I have one I'd like you to use. It's one I always use with students. I'll take a look at your fishing rod later. You inherited it, right?"

"Yes, from my grandfather. He grew up in Michigan where he learned to fly-fish, and he would go back there on vacations. My dad wasn't a fisherman though, so I never really learned. Grandpa was the one who took me fishing with my cane pole and worms. I loved it. He said I was 'a natural.' But that was twenty-five years ago."

"And you haven't been since?" asked Lew.

Lisa shook her head. "'Fraid not," she said with a sheepish smile.

"Excellent," said Lew, "that means you have no bad habits to break."

\* \* \*

Before handing her new student a fly rod, Lew waited for Doc and Bruce to head upstream, which they were happy to do. "Never helps to learn something new with other people watching," said Lew, muttering so only Lisa could hear her.

When the men were out of sight, she beckoned for Lisa to walk over to where she was standing in a grassy area by the water. Holding the student rod in her right hand, Lew got started.

"The grip is critical," she said. "A good grip makes for a better cast whether you're trying to cast long or short. The key is keeping the thumb on top of the grip, because the thumb adds punch to the action from your wrist. This is what you have to remember," said Lew, demonstrating, "your thumb is the secret to adding speed and direction to your cast. Don't ever let anyone tell you otherwise."

Keeping the rod in her right hand, Lew held it out for Lisa to see as she said, "Keep the thumb flexed like this with the first section pressed against the grip and a little space under the lower section here." She held out the fly rod so Lisa could see her grip up close.

"I went to a fly-fishing school out East and learned from one of the best fly casters in the world, Joan Wulff," said Lew. "She said something that really helped me, which is to think of this grip, especially when you're doing a forward cast, as being kind of like opening a screen door where you push with your thumb and pull back with your lower fingers. Here, try it."

She handed the fly rod to Lisa and watched her grip the rod. After a couple of adjustments, Lew said, "Okay, next I'm going to show you a roll cast followed by a forward cast and a backcast, then we'll get in the water."

Lisa rolled her eyes and said, "This is a lot to remember, Chief Ferris. Maybe I should take notes?"

"The idea is you have years to practice," said Lew, her eyes dead serious. She broke into a grin. "Don't worry—it'll come. You'll be double hauling in no time."

"What's that?"

"Next week's lesson. I'm kidding—that's something you learn once you're proficient at the basics. Okay, into the water. I'm going to show you the correct way to stand as you're casting."

Lisa stepped into the river and moved forward a few steps. Her feet shot out from under her and down she went. *Whoosh!*

As she struggled to her feet, Lew grasped one arm to pull her up. "Helps to move forward keeping your weight over your feet. Even with the best wading boots, rocks can be very slippery. That's why," Lew lifted one foot to show her what she meant as she said, "these boots have felt soles—the better to grab."

Then she smiled, adding, "But, hey, Lisa, welcome to fly-fishing. If this is the only time you fill your waders, you'll be way ahead of the rest of us. Part of the fun."

"Really?" Lisa looked like she was reconsidering this adventure.

"Okay. Next lesson: stance. Again, you'll hear variations from other people, but I recommend an open stance. Keep your body sideways to the target, your feet one in front of the other with the left foot pointing at the target, the right one dropped back and turned out at a ninety-degree angle. If you're a tennis player, this is identical to how you stand when serving. With your rod angled out about forty-five degrees, you are ready to cast, and the heart of the cast, as Joan Wulff has famously said, is this power snap, which is just what it sounds like and moves your fly line from one side of the rod to the other."

With those words, Lew demonstrated what she meant on a backcast and a forward cast, saying, "This may take a while to learn, but don't worry, just keep your elbow close to your body—and we're cooking!"

With a determined look, Lisa got started. Every time she did it wrong, Lew repeated, "Keep the elbow close to the body." After twenty minutes, she put a hand on Lisa's shoulder and said, "That's good to start. Just remember: keep the elbow close to the body. And do not listen to any guys who think they know better. Understood?" Lisa gave her a thumbs-up.

A few minutes later, Doc and Bruce came back around the upstream bend, casting as they moved along.

"Watch Doc," said Lew. "See how he's using that power snap, keeping his elbow in tight to his body?" Lisa nodded. "Doc had never fly-fished before we met so, like you, no bad habits, though he's a longtime musky fisherman. Bruce, on the other hand . . ."

Lisa watched as Bruce had executed a backcast with his elbow up and away from his body. "I'm trying to beat it out of him," said Lew. "Not sure if he'll ever learn, but he does try. Problem is he's been casting that way since he was twelve. He's trying to change, but that movement is so ingrained that it's unconscious."

"Is that why he loves to fish with you? Because you make him feel bad?" Lisa laughed.

"I wouldn't work with him if I didn't know that he's trying. With all his heart he is trying." Lew lowered her voice. "What I don't tell him is, bad cast or no, he will still catch fish. But it can be easier if you do it right."

She called out to the two men as they were trying to cast under the branches of tag alders hanging over the water. "Hey, you two," said Lew. "Time for cheese and crackers. Let's take a break."

Pulling a small picnic basket from the passenger seat of her truck, Lew walked over to where everyone had sat down on the grass. She spread out a newspaper and unloaded a brick of cheddar cheese and a small paring knife, a plastic bag filled with crackers, and another bag stuffed with cookies.

"Dive in, folks," said Lew as she cut herself a slice of cheese. She was surprised how hungry she was until she realized it was nearly three and she had forgotten to eat lunch.

"When do you have time to bake?" asked Lisa, chomping on a molasses cookie.

"I don't," said Lew with a smile. "These are from the Loon Lake Bakery and a little stale, as they've been in

Nellie—that's my truck—since Doc and I got some fishing in last week."

"Any luck?" asked Bruce who had devoured half the brick of cheese.

"Ah, glad you asked," said Lew. "Doc, you want to answer that?"

"She did, I didn't."

"And why was that?" Lew teased him.

"She told me I could better match the hatch we had that evening if I used a Royal Wulff but I wanted to use my tried-and-true Woolly Bugger."

"And he refused to change trout flies. Men," Lew snorted.

Osborne waved away the insult. "I wanted to try it because our brilliant fly fisherman here tied it herself and gave it to me as a birthday gift."

"With no guarantees," said Lew.

"So how do you decide what trout fly to use?" asked Lisa. "I was in a sporting goods store in Wausau the other day and I swear they have a million trout flies."

"Okay, let's talk about that," said Lew as she put away the few remaining crackers and picked up the newspaper. Cheese and cookies had disappeared. "I have a rock solid rule when it comes to going into the stream with trout flies. Bruce, please show Lisa what not to do."

Astonishment on his face, Bruce sputtered as he reached into three of the pockets of his fly-fishing vest.

With a sheepish expression on his face, he pulled out three plastic boxes, each holding at least a dozen trout flies.

"How did you know?" he asked Lew.

"Bruce, how long have I been instructing you?"

"Two years now, maybe a little longer."

Lew turned to Lisa, shaking her head. "He is coming around. He used to carry as many as six boxes. Here's my rule," Lew went on as she pulled a small plastic case from one of the pockets on her fishing vest. "Given you are trying to use a fly that matches whatever insect is hatching at the time so the fish decides to feed on your trout fly instead of the live bug, I say never have more than five trout flies from which to choose. Five. No more. And I'll show you what I mean. Here in the Northwoods of Wisconsin we know the weather and the insects native to this area, so it's not that difficult to choose what's most likely to raise a fish at a given time." She paused to open the little box and hold it out so Lisa could see.

"My choice of five trout flies rarely differs, and the five are this Royal Wulff, these two tiny Blue Olives, which are on number twenty-two and number twenty-four hooks respectively, one Pale Morning Dun, and," she winked, "I always have one outrageous Salmon Stone Fly, which is a fluffy bugger, just in case."

"Just in case?"

"You never know for sure what you might see out on the river. With these five, you are prepared."

"Whoa, this is a lot to process," said Lisa looking overwhelmed. "Like getting all of grad school in one day."

"Good reason to come back for more," said Doc. "Isn't too difficult to twist Lew's arm to get her out on the water."

"But I have one question, Chief Ferris," said Lisa. "The fly rod from my grandfather. Should I start using that?"

"Not yet. You said it's bamboo, right?" Lisa nodded. "I suggest you take your bamboo rod to Ralph's Sporting Goods in Loon Lake and ask Ralph to check it over. He's an expert when it comes to both graphite and bamboo rods. If he has questions or if it needs repair, he'll send it off to experts. And I'm sure he can fix that dented case too. But, Lisa, when it comes to choosing the right rod for yourself, what you need to look for is one that feels right when you cast. That's why you should spend more time learning technique. Once you have a better sense of what you're doing, then you can try different fly rods. You want to find the one that feels like an extension of your own arm."

"Sounds challenging," said Lisa, raising her eyebrows.

"Not at all. You'll know in an instant."

"Okay, then—so how soon can I have my next lesson?" Lisa grinned.

"Smart woman," said Bruce as he broke down his rod and slipped it into its case.

"Sometime next week maybe," said Lew. "I have a lot on my plate, but I promise we'll do it again."

Twenty minutes later, Lew found herself driving Nellie home and humming to Paul Simon on the radio.

# Chapter Fifteen

It was surprisingly warm for a late afternoon in mid-May. The two boys, deliriously happy that it was Saturday and no school, had messed around in the woods all afternoon. First they crawled inside the gaping trunk of a fallen hemlock where one of them insisted a bear had spent the winter.

"We could do it, too," said Alvin. "Just bring a couple blankets, a little camp stove. Plenty of room in here, and we can close the opening with branches. We can hide. No one will know we're here." He giggled.

His friend thought that over. "What about eating? We'd have to leave all the time to get food, and how about all the snow? My dad said we got six feet of snow last winter."

"Yeah," said Alvin, "hadn't thought about that. Bears don't need to eat all winter 'cause they hibernate and sleep. Oh well."

"Yeah. And what if the bear who sleeps here wants his place back?"

Alvin nodded. *Good point.*

Then they broke off branches they could use to try and knock down an eagle's nest they'd spotted in a tree down near the river. But the nest was so high it was as if the eagles had known two rowdy ten-year-olds were coming. After jumping and missing and finding it impossible to climb high enough in the tree holding the nest, the boys gave up.

One of the boys had stuck two Hershey bars into his jacket pocket. He pulled them out, and the two of them sat on a rotting log to enjoy the chocolate.

"Hey, man, look over there," said Robbie, the second boy, pointing through a screen of young aspen and balsam. His buddy leaned forward to peer in the direction he was pointing.

"I don't see nothin', why?"

Robbie chewed his last square of chocolate and stood up. "I dunno, I see something white. C'mon, let's see what it is."

Reluctant to finish his candy bar too fast, Alvin stayed right where he was and watched his friend push through low-hanging branches.

"It's over there," said Robbie who had almost disappeared into the dense brush that had grown up under the pines studding the land across the road from his grandfather's house on the Pelican River. Most of the land around there belonged to the McDonoughs but no one ever enforced the "No Trespassing" signs, so Robbie considered the property his to explore.

Robbie's great-grandfather, Robert Willis, had purchased land nearby from a railroad company back in the late 1800s and logged it occasionally up until his death. The Willis acres, along with those belonging to the McDonoughs, were among the few that still held old-growth timber and elegant, ancient hemlocks, though the old trees were being crowded out by younger ones. Since the crazed logging era, the red pine, white pine, and balsam had recovered with such fervor that the plundering of the forests of northern Wisconsin by logging barons a hundred-plus years ago had been forgotten by most people living there now.

Dragging his feet, Alvin followed Robbie into the brush, pushing branches out of the way before he got stabbed in the eye.

"Let's go home," said Alvin in a whine. It had been a fun, long afternoon and he was hungry. The candy bar had sparked a sudden desire for a liverwurst sandwich and his grandma's chocolate chip cookies.

"Ohmygosh—look at that." Excited, Robbie was hopping up and down. He had stumbled into a small clearing in front of an old shack, its roof draped with dirty gray sheets that hung over walls of weathered slab wood. "How 'bout we make this our very own?" He waved at Alvin, who was fighting his way through to the clearing. "Like, we have our own fort or something, y'know."

At the sight of the dilapidated structure, Alvin perked up. "Yeah, this can be our deer camp—just you and me, no one else." His big brothers had a deer camp and kept insisting he was too young to hunt. He'd show them. "Who owns this place?"

"I dunno. Must be my family if we own this land, but I've never seen it before. Let's look inside."

At first the boys poked around the old shack, not sure which of them was brave enough to go in first. They found one window too dark to see through and an old wooden door hanging on one rusty hinge. The door was half closed.

Robbie pulled on it and the door fell off the hinge, knocking him down. Getting to his feet, he followed Alvin through the opening. A weak ray of sunlight worked its way through the dusty, darkened window at the back of the one-room hut. Through the shadows, they could barely make out a small gray bundle in one corner.

"Careful," said Robbie, "looks like a dead animal. Probably smelly and awful. Don't get too close. Let me get a stick or something." He backed out and looked around for a stick. Finding one, he went back in and edged his way closer to the heap in the corner. A mouse scurried out and Robbie leapt back with a yelp as Alvin gave a high-pitched strangled laugh.

Both boys calmed down, breathing deeply as Robbie crept closer again. He was about to poke it when he realized he was looking at something wearing clothes.

"Alvin," he said hesitantly, "this might be a person all balled up."

Alvin tiptoed closer. He took the branch from Robbie and pushed at the mound. It rolled off to one side and unfolded. The face was gone.

The boys screamed and ran. Outside the shack, they stood screaming and screaming until they realized no one could hear them. With no path in sight, they didn't know which way to go. "Why isn't there a way out of here?" cried Alvin.

"I don't know," said Robbie, feeling close to tears. "We're in the woods, remember." He stopped to think about where they had been messing around all afternoon.

"Okay. I know. Let's go back down to the river. Then we can walk to our bikes and get help."

They got to Robbie's house first, and his big brother, Butch, on hearing their story just laughed. "You kids been doing mushrooms?"

\* \* \*

Officer Adamczak got the call. He drove out to the home of Robbie's parents and listened to what the boys said they had found. He didn't like the sound of it. Roger Adamczak was terrified of dead bodies—*another reason you should never have taken this job*, he told himself, and for the umpteenth time added up the number of days until he could retire. He decided to call Chief Ferris for instructions.

Lew answered the call just as she and Doc were finishing up the early dinner she had cooked to celebrate a pleasant afternoon spent in the river. The duck she roasted had been a gift from Ray, and the apple pie had come out of the freezer half-baked and ready to be cooked the rest of the way. Osborne, feeling satisfied and happy with his life, sat back to watch his favorite cook as she took her last forkful of pie while listening to her officer on duty. Once off the phone, she glanced down at her watch. "Well, Doc, it's definitely a Saturday night Happy Hour somewhere. What do we think our friendly coroner is up to right now?"

It was still light when Lew and Doc pulled up at the home of Robbie's parents. Officer Adamczak was there too.

"I'm so sorry, Chief," he said. "I drove down to where the boys came out of the woods on their bikes, but I couldn't quite figure out where the heck the shack is. I walked in a ways and didn't see anything."

Lew had an APP on her department cell phone that Dani had recently installed and shown her how to use. Lew pulled it up. "This is similar to Google Maps and it's designed for hunters," she explained to George Willis, Robbie's father, who was watching her. "It'll show me the forest land in detail, and it specifies whether the land is public or private—and, if private, who owns it. If I can find the shack on here, then we can figure out a way in."

Minutes later she had the building on the tiny screen, and pulling back she saw a way in. "Apparently it's on McDonough property," she said, "and I see an old logging lane coming in from County Y over here . . ."

"I know right where that is," said George. "I've hunted grouse down that way. I don't remember seeing any building though. Can you tell how far in?"

"Maybe a quarter mile, probably just far enough you can't see it from the road," said Lew.

"If a tree hasn't fallen on that old logging lane, we should be able to drive down there," said George. "Why don't you follow my truck in case we run into hazards of some kind. The truck is indestructible but your police car may not be." He gave a grim smile.

\* \* \*

Her hands encased in nitrile gloves, Lew leaned over the body and gently prodded the back pockets of the victim's dark-gray jeans. She pulled out a small, flat leather credit-card case. Getting to her feet, she reached gingerly for the driver's license.

"Noah McDonough," she said softly. "Doc, you next. While you're busy, I'll see if I can reach our soon-to-have-his-dinner-ruined favorite of the Wausau Boys."

A minute later, Bruce was looking over at Lisa Carter, with whom he was having a beer at the bar in the Loon Lake Inn as he said, "Good thing you booked a room for the night, kiddo. Let's hope the kitchen here serves late."

As they hurried out to his SUV, Bruce said, "Chief Ferris just sent me directions. Take us 'bout fifteen minutes to get there."

It was dark when they arrived, and the light from four flashlights and a good-sized lantern borrowed from Robbie's father made it easy enough for Lisa to see the body, but that was all. While she did a preliminary exam, Lew called for the EMTs from St. Mary's Hospital to move the body to the hospital morgue until morning.

Bruce took over securing the area so there would be nothing disturbed until he could get his crew up from the Wausau Crime Lab early in the morning. "Pray there's no drug bust tonight so we can get right on it then. Be difficult to work this area tonight, and there's no rain in the forecast. I'd feel better working in good light."

He was apologizing to Lew for the delay when Lisa overheard him and said, "The body has been here at least two days, Chief Ferris. With no bad weather forecast, that should be okay. Moving the body tonight is important though. You can see from the head that some animals have already damaged the remains."

# Chapter Sixteen

～

Sunday was not the quiet day Lew had hoped for. Besieged with calls from the Rhinelander newspaper and television station, she decided to hold a press conference. With Bruce Peters beside her, she opened by explaining that the Wausau Crime Lab had been brought in to handle the investigation. She went on to tell the two newspaper reporters and the anchor with the television crew what was known and not known.

"The unfortunate situation at the moment is that Grace McDonough, a longtime summer resident of Loon Lake whose family is highly respected in our community, and her twenty-four-year-old son, Noah, are deceased. The victims were discovered in different locations, and we do not have any details yet as to the cause of death for either victim. We will update you when we know."

"Chief Ferris," said one reporter, a woman from the Rhinelander television station, "we know that Ms. McDonough's son did not appear for a scheduled jail bond hearing. Do you have reason to believe he committed suicide?"

"Until we receive the autopsy reports on both victims, we have no idea of the cause of death. Mr. Peters, do you have anything to add?"

"No," said Bruce. "The investigation is ongoing and we will keep you updated."

"I have a question," said a young man from the local newspaper, "I heard that the retired professor Dr. Peter Ferris might be the victim of foul play. Are the McDonough deaths related?"

Bruce stifled a look of surprise before saying: "We don't know the full details of his death yet. Again, let me underscore what I said a minute ago—we will keep you updated. Chief Ferris?" He turned to Lew.

"Thank you, everyone," said Lew, making it clear the press conference was over. None of the reporters standing in front of her looked satisfied. One approached her with more questions, but she shooed him away.

\* \* \*

After staring at the paperwork piling up on her desk, Lew took action: she decided that, as it was Sunday, she could hide out at home. Take time to think. She called the one person who was expecting her. "Erin, I need to apologize, but I'm in no mood to go door to door for our campaign today."

"I'm not surprised," said Erin. "Dad told me about the boys finding Noah McDonough. What a strange time. I think it's wise not to knock on doors today too. People will bug you for more news about the deaths, which you don't need right now. Let's plan next weekend instead. But one piece of good news, which is Ralph's Sporting Goods is insisting on making a nice donation to the campaign."

"Oh, that's very nice," said Lew. After ending the call, she thought, *Great. Next thing Ralph will be arrested for cooking meth and I'll have a conflict of interest.* She told herself to forget it and go home.

Collapsing on the small leather sofa where she loved to sit and read, a knock on the door surprised her. "Bridget," she said, opening the door to her niece, "you didn't tell me you were coming. Please come in," and Lew welcomed her with a hug.

"Aunt Lew," Bridget said. "Didn't Linda tell you they returned Dad's body yesterday and she's arranged a memorial service for tomorrow morning?"

Lew was stunned.

"Oh, I can see from your face you didn't know."

Shrugging, Lew closed the door behind Bridget. "That's Linda. Would you like to stay here tonight? You can have Suzanne's room."

"I would love that," said Bridget. "When I hadn't heard from you, I reserved a room at the Loon Lake Inn—"

"Cancel it," said Lew. "Now you know why you didn't hear. Please, sit down at the kitchen table. Are you hungry?"

"Very. I drove up from Madison without stopping."

When Bridget had finished eating the ham and cheese sandwich Lew made for her, she stood up, set her dishes in the sink, and said, "I'm going to run into town and stop by Dad's. If it's okay with Linda, I want to get hold of his address book so I can let a few of his friends know about tomorrow. If she didn't tell you, I'm sure she hasn't told them. Do you want to come with me?"

"I'll stay here if that's okay," said Lew. "I haven't done a load of wash in days and it's getting serious. Call me if you need me, but otherwise I'll see you later."

*　*　*

As Bridget drove up to her childhood home, which her father had shared with his second wife, she was relieved to see no car in the driveway. She knocked on the front door but there was no answer. Using a key she'd had since childhood, she let herself in the door off the patio behind the house.

Once inside, she went to her father's den. "What on earth?" she exclaimed to herself. File folders and loose papers were strewn across the desk and all over the floor. Her father had two small metal file cabinets on each side of his desk. The drawers had been pulled out of the cabinets and the files dumped on the floor. Someone had been searching for something.

Checking the desk, she pulled open the second drawer on the left, which was where her dad had always kept his address book and a checkbook. They were there. *Whew!* she thought. She stuffed both into her purse. She knew she probably shouldn't take the checkbook but decided to anyway. Remembering what her dad had said about Linda and the affair, she knew she would feel better if she showed it to Lew before returning it. Maybe Linda wasn't entitled to it anyway. Maybe she didn't even know it existed.

Kneeling, Bridget started to gather up the scattered files. The first group included study plans from when her father was teaching, along with files on individual students. She knew he had kept those in case students needed references for graduate school or jobs. She put those back in the file cabinet. Then there were files relating to his work with Loon Rescue. She returned those to the second file cabinet.

She was about to leave when she decided to take a quick look through the rest of his desk drawers. She sat down, but before opening a drawer she remembered that her dad kept a safe in the closet. A few years ago he had shown her what he kept in the safe: a few pieces of jewelry and other memorabilia, including an album of photos from his wedding to her mother. She decided she better grab that before Linda discovered the jewelry, which Bridget suspected she would keep, and the album, which she would probably throw away.

The safe combination was the date she was born—her birthday. She smiled, remembering the day her father had shared that with her. She opened the safe and reached in. The album was there, and a small case holding her mother's garnet bracelet and matching earrings. Her dad had tried to give those to her after the funeral, but she was afraid they could get lost or stolen if she took them to school and had asked him to hold onto them for safekeeping.

She was surprised to find one more item: a thick brown envelope file fastened with an elastic tie. On opening the envelope, she discovered legal papers of some kind. She decided to hold on to the envelope too and slipped it into her backpack. She was getting to her feet when the door to the den slammed open.

"What the hell are you doing?" The man shouting at her looked familiar. Linda was standing behind him.

"Stan, take it easy," said Linda. "This is Bridget, Pete's daughter."

"She has no business going through things here," Bridget heard the man say.

"You have no business shouting at me," said Bridget, keeping her voice even in spite of her anger. "Who made the mess in here, Linda? Dad's files were thrown everywhere. I put them back where they belong. And for the record, Linda, Dad's things in here are not yours. I want the school records and his notes on the environment and everything." She waved her arm around the room, relieved that she had closed the safe and the door to the closet before the two appeared.

"Stan," said Linda, "I thought I told you to put those files back when you were done."

"What did you want with those?" Bridget asked the heavyset man, whom she now realized must be the guy her dad thought Linda was having an affair with. "I'm sure Linda knows where the financial records are." She locked eyes with Linda. "That's why you married him, isn't it?"

As soon as she said it, Bridget knew that she was out of line and better leave fast.

Linda's eyes darkened. "Get out of my house."

"Going, going, going," said Bridget in a singsong voice as she backed out of the room, then walked slowly, deliberately down the hall and out the front door.

At least they hadn't parked behind her car.

She backed out of the driveway, drove down two blocks, pulled over, put the car in Park and broke down.

# Chapter Seventeen

〜

"Mom always said these were the color of dragon's blood," said Bridget after wiping away her tears. She held up the bracelet, a half-inch-wide band of eighteen-caret gold, barely large enough to encircle her slim wrist and encrusted with dark-red garnets. The matching earrings were simple: one large garnet set in gold and designed to be worn against the earlobe.

"These are lovely," said her aunt. "I'm glad you were able to find them." She smiled reassuringly, relieved to see Bridget was calming down.

The girl had arrived back at Lew's place with tears running down her face. At first Lew thought it was the impact of walking into her family home and knowing her father would not be there.

She was wrong.

"Linda had this horrible man with her. Fat, loud— God almighty, Aunt Lew, Dad's only been dead . . ."

She couldn't finish and collapsed sobbing in Lew's arms. When she could take a deep breath, Lew said, "Can you talk about it?" More deep breaths. "Tell me what happened. Talking about it—you'll feel better."

"Okay." After blowing her nose, Bridget tried to wipe her tears away but gave up. "I got there. Linda wasn't home so I let myself in and went right to Dad's den. I wanted his address book, but the place was a mess, with Dad's files dumped on the floor and scattered everywhere."

Bridget wiped her nose. "Aunt Lew, it really looked like someone had been searching for something. I mean why would they throw stuff around like that? I picked everything up because I know how neat Dad is."

Lew noticed that Bridget was speaking of her father in the present tense. She squeezed her shoulder as she tried not to cry herself.

"When I had everything put back together, I got the address book out of his desk." Bridget paused. "And I did a bad thing, maybe 'cause I, um, took a checkbook that was right there, too. Better give that back, huh?"

"We'll wait on that," said Lew. "Show it to me first. Who knows? Could be a checkbook for Loon Rescue and we should give it to them. Your dad was on a couple boards, you know."

Bridget relaxed a little at that. "Yeah, I haven't looked at it. Then I remembered the safe, so I found it in the closet where Dad's always kept it and got my jewelry box."

"Oh," Lew was surprised, "so the safe wasn't locked?"

"It was, but Dad told me the combination a long time ago—the date of my birthday. Maybe I shouldn't have done that?"

"You still have your bedroom in your dad's house, right? I mean, you could be staying there tonight instead of my place—right?"

"Yes, but please don't—"

"No, that's not my point," said Lew. "My point is that your Dad's house has been your home even after his second marriage. Your things are there—clothes, books, stuff from childhood. The jewelry is yours because your dad gave it to you, and you had the right to open the safe because, again, your dad made that clear when he gave you the combination."

Bridget nodded. "So . . . then . . . you think it's okay if I took something else?" She reached into her backpack and pulled out the large brown envelope. She loosened the elastic tie and let the papers inside slide out onto her lap.

"What are those?" asked Lew. "His will?"

"No, and I haven't looked at any of 'em yet."

Sitting side by side on Lew's small leather loveseat, the two of them studied the pages as Bridget had handed them over, one by one, to Lew.

"These are research reports on something," said Lew. "Ah, I see—look at this one." She handed two pages clipped together to Bridget, saying, "These are scientific studies documenting the effects of sulfide mining on different bodies of water . . . here in the U.S.A. and abroad."

She was quiet as she continued to study the contents. When she had finished, she glanced back at the top of the first page, where was startled to see the name of a man she knew well, one of Pete's close friends and a lawyer from Rhinelander. Setting the pages in her lap, Lew turned to Bridget.

"The top two pages are a memo to your dad detailing a lawsuit this lawyer is planning to file." Lew looked up from the page and added, "a lawsuit that is going to be filed sometime soon. Your dad is one of the people behind the lawsuit. Let me see that checkbook you found."

Bridget reached into her purse for the checkbook, which she held out to Lew. Lew saw at a glance there were only a few entries. "This is a checkbook that belongs to an organization called The Pelican River Action Committee, and this is money collected to pay the legal fees for the lawsuit.

"So you did fine, Bridget. You didn't take anything personal that might belong to Linda. I wouldn't worry about it. Just return the checkbook to your dad's lawyer friend with whom he was working on the project and everything should be fine. Quite frankly, good thing you found it. Who knows what Linda would have done with it."

"Aunt Lew," said Bridget said with funny little grin, the grin of a person who knows she did a bad thing but doesn't regret it one iota, "'Fraid I haven't told you everything I did . . ."

"Hmm, do I want to hear this?" asked her aunt, reading mischief on her niece's face. "Remember, I *am* an officer of the law."

"It's not that bad—I don't think."

With that Bridget described being caught in the room by a strange man who yelled at her.

". . . And I shouted right back. Linda was standing behind him too, so she heard me. She said something that made me think she'd asked him to look at Dad's files."

"Do you know who this was?"

"No, but I know I've seen him somewhere before. He's big and fat, you know, the kind whose stomach enters the room before they do. She called him Stan."

"There's only one Stan around Loon Lake these days," said Lew. "Stan Mayer. I wonder what he was doing there?"

"I think he's the one she's having the affair with," said Bridget. "Wherever they were before they got there, they were in one car. And I could smell alcohol real strong when he kind of loomed over me." She shivered.

After mulling over Bridget's words, Lew handed her the papers from the brown envelope saying: "Let's put these in a safe place. The lawyer's name is on the first page and I'll bet he's in your dad's address book. Did Linda tell you what time the memorial service is? She's probably planning to call me at the last minute and hope I don't show up."

"Yes, it's at eleven at the funeral home."

"Okay, let's share the names in the address book and start calling. Let's surprise Linda with a good gathering."

"Oh, Aunt Lew, I love that!" Bridget jumped up and grabbed her cell phone from her purse.

"You work at the kitchen table, I'll be at my desk here," said Lew. "And when we're done, I'll order us a pizza."

\*    \*    \*

An hour later, they had reached most of Pete's friends with Loon Rescue as well as former colleagues from the college, several former students with whom he'd stayed in touch, and the four people involved in the Pelican River Action Committee, including the lawyer who had written the memo, Rich Hartman.

Lew called him, but before she could say anything, he said, "Chief Ferris, I am heartbroken. When I got the news of Pete's heart attack—"

"Rich, stop right there," said Lew. "This is still confidential, but there was no heart attack. My brother was murdered. I don't know by whom yet but I will find the person. Trust me."

After a short pause, Rich said, "I wonder if it's related to our work against the mining operation. We were trying to keep a lid on our work until we could get this lawsuit filed. We had hoped to do that as early as next week . . ."

"I have your memo and the reports on the pollution that sulfide mining can cause. Do you need Pete's files back? Also, we have the checkbook belonging to your organization."

"Yes, I would appreciate that but, one more question, do you think his daughter—and his wife—would mind if I say a few words tomorrow? Pete was a close friend of mine."

"I'll have Bridget introduce you," said Lew. She didn't mention Linda. She didn't care if Linda minded or not.

*　*　*

Lying in bed later that night, Lew found herself wide-awake and thinking about Stan Mayer. What could he have been looking for in Pete's files? The only thing that made sense was the information about the anti-mine group. But why?

Stan had no financial interest in that. Nor, for that matter, did Linda. At least not as far as Lew knew. On the other hand, maybe Stan had stock in the mining company. But he was a real-estate appraiser, not even a realtor.

Normandy Mining had appeared out of nowhere, and so recently that Lew doubted many people living in Loon Lake were familiar with the company. On the other hand, maybe company executives had courted local people, prominent people, to push their agenda. But Stan Mayer wasn't exactly a pillar of the community. He had a small appraisal business and he drank too much. That was Stan.

Lew knew she was prejudiced. After all, she had gone all through grade school and high school with the boor. She felt differently about his former wife, Charlotte. She had married Stan right out of high school when he was still basking in the glory of having been a star football player and she was a cheerleader.

The marriage had lasted three years, long enough to produce young John, who, as far as Lew knew, was a good kid and a good friend of Doc's granddaughter, Mason. She found the kids to be bright and funny and good-hearted even if they did come up with horrible ideas like luring a sex predator into a citizen's arrest.

As she was drifting off, Lew thought about Charlotte, John's mom. The divorce from Stan had been the best thing that ever happened to that woman. Even as she had worked days as a CNA, she had gone back to school for a degree in nursing and today ran the public health department for the county.

No, Charlotte was no slouch, and she was definitely not fat.

On that note Lew fell sound asleep.

# Chapter Eighteen

It was 7 AM on Monday, and Osborne, legs crossed and sipping his second cup of coffee, was relaxing back in his chair alongside five of his buddies at McDonald's. Two of the guys were in the midst of recounting how they had survived the freak snowstorm on opening day of fishing at the Rainbow Flowage, when Steve Keron, a newbie to the group and a soon-to-be-retired banker, strolled in.

He smirked at his friends as he sat down, cupped his hands around a mug of hot coffee, leaned back to stretch out his long legs—and said nothing.

Everyone stared at him.

"Okay, what?" asked Herm, the elder of the group.

"Got a little piece of news that I can finally talk about," said Steve, again with the smirk. Throats cleared and chairs scraped as the table came to attention. When he was sure they were ready, Steve pulled his legs back under him and sat up straight. Leaning over with his elbows on the table, he lowered his voice so nearby customers would have to strain to overhear.

"Ol' Stan Mayer is about to become a very rich man," he said, and checked faces to be sure everyone knew who he was talking about. They did.

"Just before she died in that car accident last Friday?" he said, raising his voice as if asking a question, "Grace McDonough made him her right-hand man to broker a deal selling a humongous chunk of her land to Normandy Mining. Old Stan gets twenty-five percent of whatever he can negotiate. And, trust me, those will be b-i-i-g bucks."

"He can't do that," said Herm. "He's not a licensed realtor."

"Doesn't matter. Grace made him her partner on the deal. I guess Stan was able to persuade her that he could wring more money out of the mining company than any realtor could.

"Now we all know Stan—he'll fudge the numbers on anything if there's a buck in it for him. The two of them were in our bank last Wednesday, and she signed off on their agreement. We have the McDonough Trust, which is why we're involved."

"So what's that land worth?" asked Osborne.

"Well, one piece of the property—the land along the Pelican—was appraised last year at a couple hundred grand. Guess who did that appraisal?" Everyone nodded.

"Yep, Stan, of course. We approved a modest mortgage, and six months later when Stan found that Normandy Mining was interested . . . Hell, he told Grace she could get two million, maybe more —*if* he helped her. He told Grace that if the Normandy Mining test drilling was successful, they'd be mining copper and nickel to the tune of many, many millions. You can imagine how Grace loved hearing that.

"Now that she's not with us, I don't mind sharing that over the past few years that woman made more than one bad bet in the stock market. She was desperate to sell some land. Stan showed up with that nice proposal at exactly the right time."

The seven men sitting at the round table sipped their coffee in silence.

Then Herm said, "So even if she's dead, he gets his twenty-five percent?"

"If her son and heir chooses to work with Stan and sell the land along the Pelican River, which is what Normandy Mining wants. Yep, it's all legal and we know Grace can't change her mind now."

"You heard they found her son's body yesterday?" asked Osborne.

"No! No, I didn't hear that." Steve shot up in his chair, stunned. "Are you kidding me? I was down in Madison over the weekend. What on earth? What's the story? Pretty strange to have both McDonoughs die."

"And no accidents," said Osborne. "The autopsy on Grace indicates foul play, and the condition in which her son's body was found . . . well, let's just say something unpleasant must have happened to that young man."

"So the question will be," said Herm, "who gets the estate? Maybe Stan isn't so lucky after all. Maybe some distant relatives could have other ideas, right?"

"Are there any distant relatives?" asked one of the guys.

"Not that I can recall," said Steve, a quizzical expression on his face. "At least not according to the estate documents I've seen. Grace was the only progeny of the old man and Noah her only child. She had the kid out of wedlock and never married, so no complications there." He sat quietly, thinking.

"I believe," he said, speaking slowly, "in a situation like this the bank assumes trusteeship. Trusts generally put language in place in the event that all family members are deceased. I'll have to check into that."

"How long until you retire?—maybe you and the bank can get twenty-five percent," said Herm.

"I wish," said Steve with a grin. "Doubt it though. Me? I got four weeks left, then you will be honored with my presence here at the esteemed McDonald's every morning—most mornings anyway. And I can't wait."

\* \* \*

Even as Doc and his buddies were gossiping over their coffee, Lew had arrived at the Loon Lake police department to find Ray waiting for her. Slouching comfortably in one of the upholstered chairs in front of her desk, he was holding a small Ziploc bag, which he held up as she walked in.

"All I could find," he said as he set the bag down in front of her.

Lew walked over and looked down at three cigarette butts. "From Lynn Lake?"

"Yep, Chief, I've . . ." Lew waited through the long, irritating pause so typical of Ray when he had important information, "been back there . . . twice. Now . . .," he took a deep breath, "Doc said you needed yesterday off or . . . I would have gotten . . . ," he leaned forward, "this to you sooner."

"He was right, and thank you," said Lew, pulling her chair out to sit down. She wanted to add that it usually takes at least a day to recover from losing one of the people you love most. But she knew Ray knew.

"I checked . . . every . . . single . . . inch of Wolf Hollow. Didn't find . . . a leaf chewed or . . . an acorn crushed until . . . I walked up this berm 'bout fifty yards from the parking lot . . . place is covered with sumac bushes." Now he sat up a little straighter. "Covered, so it's . . . easy . . . to hide if you need to. And you can park on Stella Road and walk over without being seen . . . not by someone coming from the east like your brother."

Ray picked up speed as he went on: "Standing on top of the berm you can see the parking lot and . . . right down to where the path to the loon nest starts. Made sense to me . . . that someone might . . . have waited there—and that is where . . . I found these butts. Worth having the Wausau boys check for DNA, doncha think?"

"Damn right," said Lew. "Good work. Between these and that pry bar we might have something."

Ray, pointing his left index finger, said, "I have . . . one more suggestion . . . if you don't mind, Chief."

Lew gave him an encouraging look. "Go right ahead."

"I know the guys working with Bruce Peters . . . are going through the McDonough house . . . and their cars . . . and that old shack, but . . . I'd sure like to be the one to check out the woods around the shack . . . and that old hemlock forest that runs along the river back in there. I'm sure those boys have been over every inch of the rest of the property but . . ."

"Please, good idea, Ray. I was planning to call you this morning and suggest you do exactly that. Think about it: even if Noah was killed somewhere else, how did his body get in the shack? No one has eyes better than you do, so yeah, keep track of your hours and let's hope you find something. Meantime, I'll get these butts off to the crime lab. What I can't figure is why kill both of the McDonoughs? Who were they hurting? Grace was obnoxious, sure, but harmless. Now Noah . . ."

Lew paused. "Dani hasn't found anything on his cell phone other than the incident the other day. We know his mother was able to have his California arrests classified as misdemeanors or minor offenses. While none of that is good, we have no evidence that he ever assaulted someone and didn't get caught. On the other hand, there could be an angry parent from out of town, someone whose daughter was victimized, and when that parent confronted Noah or his mother, they got the same brush-off I got?" She was quiet, thinking.

Ray, too. "I don't . . . know . . . Chief," he said after a long minute. "Loon Lake is small enough that . . . if there were strangers in town, someone may have noticed them. I'll ask around."

"Please, do that. But, Ray," she gave him a slight smile. "I do have an unrelated suggestion for you. Remember meeting the new pathologist working with the Wausau boys? Dr. Carter?"

"She called me last night," said Ray. "I'm guiding her this evening." No pauses in his conversation now. Curious how that happened when Ray's life turned serious. "She said she's got a report for you, so she'll be driving up this afternoon and will stay over at the inn. She wants a lesson on how to use a spinning rod so she can decide if she wants to fish musky or trout."

"Ah," said Lew, standing up to walk him to the office door. She didn't add what she was thinking: *decide if she wants to fish for musky or trout—or a tall, good-looking fishing guide.* Instead, she pushed Ray out the door saying, "Keep me posted."

Then she checked her watch. She had a couple of hours until she needed to walk over to the funeral home. Her phone rang.

"Family call," said Marlaine, in a blunt tone that signaled who was on the line.

"Good morning, Linda, are you doing okay?" Lew tried to sound sympathetic rather than furious, which is what the woman deserved. She listened as Linda made an excuse for the unexpectedly sudden memorial service.

When she had finished, Lew said, "I understand. Bridget gave me the news last night. I'll be there. Thank you."

She didn't let on that a good fifteen friends of Pete's would be there too, including his lawyer friend, Rich Hartman. Whatever Linda's plan might have been, she and Bridget had made sure it was theirs, not hers. And if she didn't like it? Too bad.

# Chapter Nineteen

Arriving at the entrance to the funeral home, Lew nearly collided with Dave Francis, the funeral director, as he was charging through the doorway, a frantic expression on his face. "Oh, gosh, sorry, Chief Ferris." He backed away, saying, "Please excuse me—did I step on your foot?"

"Not yet, I'm fine," said Lew, smiling so he wouldn't be too embarrassed. "Do you need help?"

"I have to get more coffee and doughnuts. Mrs. Ferris told me there would be only four people here including Father Gleason and your family. But I've got ten people already and I'm told more are coming. You know that she's the one who insisted on doing this today, right? I'm not sure I'll have the deceased's ashes back from the crematorium. This request meant those folks had to work Sunday. I hope you know they're doing their best. We all are." And he heaved a big sigh.

"Not your fault, Dave. I understand. Did she say why the service had to be so soon?"

"Something about having to leave town. She has to be somewhere tomorrow."

"So couldn't we do this later in the week maybe?"

"She wouldn't hear of it. I tried." Lew could see his frustration.

She had the same questions: Why on earth would Linda have insisted on having a memorial service so soon? Did she lack any understanding of the grief felt by Pete's family and his close friends? How selfish can a person be? It didn't make sense.

\* \* \*

But Pete's marriage to Linda never had made sense. She was so different from him, and so different from his late wife, Melanie. Physically attractive maybe, but not very bright, not much of a sense of humor. Lew's theory for why he had married her was based on observations of other marriages in which a bereaved spouse married within a year or so of losing a partner with whom they had had a long, loving relationship—a relationship grounded in friendship, in shared opinions and shared levels of understanding life's twists and turns. Relationships so comfortable they get taken for granted.

People, especially people experiencing the terrible loneliness of grief, mistakenly think those virtues can be found in anyone who seems both attractive and attentive. At first. Too late they discover the reality. The reality that Pete shared with Lew on the day he confessed with sad eyes that he would be divorcing Linda.

"I have to," he'd said. "She has no use for what I consider the important things in life, like the outdoors and wildlife, and even longtime friendships. She isn't kind . . . to me or Bridget or . . . anyone that I can tell. Frankly, Lew, kindness is not on her list of best behaviors. I think she married me thinking that because I seem to be someone prominent in town we'd have a fancy social life."

As he spoke, Pete had given Lew a silly grin and said "Me? Social? I spend half my day out on a lake staring at loons for God's sake. Plus, Lewellyn," he'd added, "the woman has no respect for good food. I mention that Ray has dropped off some of his wonderful bluegills cleaned and ready to be sautéed—and she turns white. Yep. Major life mistake made by this guy. It'll cost me but, man, it'll be worth it."

Lew had patted his shoulder and given him a sisterly hug. "I've had a few inappropriate relationships," she said to comfort him.

"Yeah, but you didn't marry 'em. And now you're with Doc. You're lucky."

Lew nodded. She was lucky and she knew it.

"So I've talked it over with Rich Hartman and he'll handle the divorce. She can have whatever money and stuff she wants." He waved a hand around his house.

And with that Lew had given her sweet, sad big brother one last hug.

Thinking back over that conversation, Lew wondered: *Is that why Linda's rushing things? Had Pete asked for the divorce and this is her revenge?*

She wouldn't put it past her.

\* \* \*

"I feel so bad rushing into this memorial service," said Dave, still standing by Lew. "So let me ask you since you're family—how many people should I buy for?"

"Figure about twenty of us," said Lew. "Linda didn't know how well Pete was liked. And none of this is your fault, Dave."

"I just wish she'd told me."

He ran down the steps and set off along the sidewalk. With McDonald's right around the corner and the bakery across the street, Lew knew he'd be back soon with plenty of refreshments.

Linda was just inside looking irritated. "Where did everyone come from?" she asked Lew. "I didn't tell anyone about this except you and Bridget."

"My fault," said Lew, "I mentioned our little gathering to a couple of friends of mine and Pete's. They probably put the word out. He was well liked, you know." She saw Bridget standing off to the side trying to hide a smile. Lew had to work hard not to smile back.

Walking past Linda into the small chapel where ashes or a casket was usually displayed, Lew saw only a vase holding three white lilies. Six chairs had been set out in front of the pedestal holding the vase, and Dave's assistant director was busy bringing in more folding chairs.

In the cluster of people standing at the back of the room Lew recognized some of Pete's friends from the college where he'd taught and volunteers from Loon Rescue. There were also a few faces she didn't recognize.

Osborne walked in with Erin's family. When he spied Lew, he headed her way and, lowering his voice, said, "You missed the look on Linda's face when the six of us walked in." He grinned conspiratorially as he added, "Thanks to you and Bridget, I think this will be a morning Pete would have very much appreciated. Any news from the Wausau boys?"

"Not yet. They have DNA off the pry bar but no match to anyone. That's all Bruce knew as of an hour ago. You know about the cigarette butts that Ray found, right?" Osborne nodded. "I got those over to Bruce just an hour ago. Oh, and Dr. Carter is meeting with me this afternoon so I'm sure I'll know more—"

"Oh, Lewellyn . . ." A voice Lew knew well interrupted them. "And Dr. Osborne, what a sad . . . how did this happen? I didn't know Pete was sick."

Lew turned to hug the woman behind the voice. Standing beside her was her son, John, who spotted his buddy Mason across the room and hurried over to join her. His mother, meanwhile, with tears in her eyes, hugged Lew back.

*   *   *

Charlotte Mayer had been the best friend of Pete's late wife, Melanie. Ten years divorced from Stan Mayer, she was now running the McBride County Public Health Department, so she and Lew crossed paths at least once a month when they had to attend Loon Lake City Council meetings. They also had offices in the same building, though the police department was on the back end and they did not share hallways.

"Oh, Charlotte," said Lew. "Thank you for coming."

"Bridget gave me the news last night." Charlotte leaned over to whisper in Lew's ear, "I'm sure Miss Linda won't appreciate my presence, but do I give a damn? Pete was one of my best friends too. And John adored him. You know Pete took him under his wing this past year and was teaching him how to build bluebird houses? As you can imagine, Stan can't be bothered."

"No, I didn't know Pete was doing that," said Lew, giving Charlotte's arm a squeeze. "Gosh, I'm glad to hear it."

For the first time since she had walked into the funeral home, Lew felt close to weeping. Charlotte's words triggered a memory of how Pete had helped her through her grief in the days after her son Chris was killed in a bar fight shortly after turning sixteen.

"John told me what happened with that McDonough guy and your meeting with the kids afterward," said Charlotte.

Struggling to keep from breaking down, Lew forced herself to listen to Charlotte, who was saying, "Sorry I had to work that afternoon, but Stan was able to be there, thank heavens. Trust me, Lew, you put the fear of God into those kids. I know my Johnny won't fool around that way again. Hey," Charlotte gave Lew another quick hug, "sorry to rattle on. You have to talk to people, but please, count on me knocking on some doors for your campaign, okay? I've already signed up with Erin." She gave a determined smile. "We need a better person for sheriff than that jack-pine savage running against you."

\* \* \*

Rich Hartman, Pete's good friend and lawyer, walked in and took a chair near the front. He was a tall man, nearly six foot seven, and built like a Green Bay Packer linesman, but a gentle soul who smiled easily. He waved to Lew, who walked over to greet him. "I'd like to say a few words when everyone's ready," he said in a low voice. "Talk a little about Pete's conservation work?"

"Sounds great to me," said Lew. "We'll get the service going shortly."

She and Bridget continued to walk around hugging people and listening as guests murmured their sympathies. Dave trotted in with a tray of doughnuts, which he set on a small table while his assistant plugged in a large coffee urn and set out cups. No sooner had the doughnuts and coffee been readied when a man rushed in with a cardboard box. "Dave, I have your delivery," he said to the funeral director. Looking relieved, Dave took the box from him and disappeared. Five minutes later he reappeared carrying a black ceramic pot with an inset lid. The image of a Great Blue Heron in flight graced the front of the elegant pot. Moving the vase with the lilies to one side, Dave set his treasure in the middle of the small pedestal.

Lew, standing nearby, heard Linda speak to the funeral director in a low voice while laying a hand on his arm as if to stop what he was doing, "Oh, my God, how much is that silly thing?"

Alarm crossed Dave's face, but Lew caught his eye and signaled.

"Paid for by one of your husband's friends," said Dave, "who wishes to remain anonymous."

"Oh," said Linda, looking disgruntled.

Later, he refused to let Lew pay for the lovely pot, saying, "I knew your brother well. He taught both my kids. Please, let me do this."

Stationing herself next to the pedestal holding her husband's ashes, Linda waited to be sure she had everyone's attention. She was looking more wizened than ever, thought Lew, with her dyed auburn hair pulled back into a straggly bun and smudged eye makeup.

"She's faking the crying," whispered Lew to Bridget, who had taken the chair beside her. Bridget poked her in the ribs.

"Shut up, Aunt Lew," she whispered back, trying to hide a smile. "You're being unkind."

"I know," said Lew, "can't help it."

"It is so dear of all of you to join me this sad morning," said Linda before launching into a too-long list of how she had treasured "wonderful, kind Peter. If only he hadn't had that stroke . . . ," she said with a catch in her voice, "but Pete died doing what he loved."

She didn't mention the pending divorce nor did she explain why she was holding the service so soon that even her late husband's ashes had arrived late. When someone in the group asked when the burial would take place, Linda replied, "No burial. I'll take care of the ashes. No reason to pay for a cemetery plot these days." The room was quiet.

"Please, Linda, you don't need to worry about that. I'll make the arrangements and let everyone know," said Lew, speaking loudly enough for the room to hear. She looked around as she declared: "Pete will be buried in our family plot at St. Mary's Cemetery near our folks and his late wife, Melanie, whom many of you knew well. He would have wanted that, and Linda understands." Several heads in the room nodded in relief.

With that, Linda gave a slight wave and said, while walking toward the back of the room, "I'm sure Lewellyn may have a few words . . ." She raised her eyebrows as she spat out the word *sure*.

Lew, ignoring the put-down, got to her feet and pulled Bridget up with her. "Thank you, Linda," she said, "but every one of you here today knew my brother very well. You wouldn't be here otherwise. For that reason, Bridget and I feel you deserve the truth. There was no stroke. Pete Ferris was murdered."

The room was still. Rich Hartman nodded his approval from where he was sitting.

"I'll be holding a press conference later today as I confirm for the public what the Wausau Crime Lab has discovered about Pete's death and several other events occurring in our community. Meanwhile, Bridget and I can't thank all of you enough for . . . for . . ." Lew lost it.

Osborne stood and walked up to put his arms around her. Bridget took over.

"Aunt Lew and I are going to be sure my father's work continues just the way he planned." Her voice was loud and firm as she leveled a stare at Linda, who was standing at the back of the room, a grim look on her face.

"I—I," Linda jerked forward stammering, then threw up her hands, saying in a loud voice, "You and Lewellyn, you are so wrong. Just like always you are goddamn wrong." With that, she turned and made a show of leaving the chapel. A door banged. She left the building. The room was quiet, all eyes on Bridget.

"I'm turning this over to our family friend Rich Hartman," said Bridget. "Everyone knows Rich, right?" A couple of people indicated they didn't, so Bridget said to Rich as he walked to the front of the room, "Can you tell everyone who you are and why you think Dad was murdered?"

"Sure," said Rich. He glanced around the room, making eye contact with the people waiting for his words. "I see many of you from our Pelican River Action Committee and I assume the rest of you who are not family members must be with Pete's Loon Rescue organization, right?" Heads nodded.

"My specialty is environmental law, and Peter Ferris—of course we all know him as Pete—was, as you know, an outstanding environmental activist dedicated to our Northwoods: our forests, our waters, our wildlife. And Pete, like myself, was keenly aware that our extraordinary life here in the Northwoods is at risk right now. At risk of pollution from the proposed Normandy Sulfide

Mine—a mine that threatens our pristine Pelican River, the life force of our Northwoods.

"Up until his death, Pete was working with me to prepare a lawsuit we had hoped to file early next week. Our lawsuit is designed to stop the Normandy Sulfide Mine test drilling along the Pelican River. If successful, we will have prevented sulfide mining from ever threatening the Pelican River.

"I won't go into details here, but you should know that Pete's research documented the pollution caused by three mines identical to the one proposed by the Normandy group. He met with the experts working to clean up the polluted rivers—it will take years—and he arranged for the documentation that should prevail in the courts and save our river.

"As he was working on this over the last six months, he was confronted on three occasions by a lawyer representing the McDonough family. As you know, up until her death Grace McDonough owned and had been planning to sell the land along the Pelican. Twice he received threatening phone calls from untraceable phone numbers. The caller was male, and Pete assumed it was probably her son Noah.

"Pete also felt that someone familiar with our work was leaking news of information we had received in confidence. So I'm asking you today—if you know who that individual is, please tell me. You can let me know in private, and I'll keep your information confidential.

"Now you can call me crazy if you wish, but I'm convinced Pete was killed by someone who does not want our lawsuit to be filed, to prevail against the proposed mine. Why?" Rich paused, "It's all about . . . money."

With his eyes on Pete's sister and daughter, Rich went on. "Lewellyn, Bridget, from all of us who are working to save the Pelican River, we owe a great debt to your brother, your father," his voice broke, "for his work, which will be key to saving our beloved river." Rich pressed his fingers against his eyelids, took a deep breath, then reached to put an arm across Bridget's shoulders. "We are so thankful to your father."

A woman whom Lew recognized as a member of Loon Rescue stood up to ask, "What about you, Rich? If Pete was killed over your lawsuit, are you in danger?"

Rich grimaced slightly as he pulled back his suit jacket to expose a holstered gun and said, "Got my concealed carry license and I know how to use this. Not too worried." A soft round of applause greeted his words, and the visitors got to their feet.

* * *

After most of the guests had left, Dave approached Lew with the black ceramic pot in his hands. "Mrs. Ferris left a while ago," he started to say.

"I'll take my brother," said Lew, smiling and reaching for the pot.

Relieved, Dave delivered the pot to her arms as Lew said, "Thank you for everything, Dave. This turned out quite nice in spite of . . ."

He grinned. "One of my more unusual services, I will say. Take care, Chief Ferris."

As she walking down the steps outside the funeral home, Lew waved good-bye to Osborne, who was headed to the parking lot with Erin and her family.

Two blocks later, nearing the Loon Lake Courthouse and her office, she noticed for the first time that spring that the lilac bushes surrounding the tall building had burst into full bloom. Inhaling their soft fragrance, she paused to let it envelop her. She sensed her brother's presence in the air around her. She felt his embrace as safe and warm as it had been that day when she was a child and they had just gotten news of their parents' deaths in a car accident on icy roads. Pete had put his arms around her, and she had known then, as now, she would be okay.

She also knew she would find the person who killed her brother.

# Chapter Twenty

Ray's battered pickup tackled the rock-strewn dirt road that led to the old shack where Noah McDonough's body had been found. Glancing down at the gap between the floorboards, he saw the space widen ever so slightly as his truck bounced along. Ray made the mental note he had been making for years: *might be time to find a new babe.*

The fact was he loved this old truck. His life history was in this vehicle. *Oops*—he had arrived.

Ray pulled off to the side where he could see the Wausau boys had been parking. The crime-scene tape securing the area around the shack had cordoned off a good ten feet surrounding the decrepit building.

*Decrepit puts it mildly,* thought Ray, whistling in amazement as he peered at the old logger's shack. Hard to believe that place was still standing. Hell, all that was visible of the roof under the filthy gray sheets that had been thrown over it were slivers of wood. Even the vertical-slab wood exterior was leaning precariously. He'd give the old place one more year at most.

*Better question: How the hell had someone found their way here in the first place?* You had to have walked the property, and why would you have done that? Hunting? Maybe, but it was private land.

Ray studied the area beyond the yellow tape looking for signs. The forest growth was too dense even for hunters. Spotting a deer trail, he stopped. Looking closer, thinking over what Chief Ferris and Bruce Peters had told him about the two kids who'd stumbled onto this place, he didn't get too excited over what he was seeing. Looked too much like where the boys had barged through to check out their discovery. Still, he couldn't be sure.

Ray followed the deer trail back through the woods to where he could see that the boys had been exploring after leaving their bikes. He saw the path leading down to the river. Yep, nothing new here. He retraced his steps to the shack.

Now he walked around to the other side, hoping to find evidence of someone other than the boys having been in the area. He wasn't sure he would, as whoever had hidden the body likely had driven up in a car or an ATV and then driven out again. But Chief Ferris wanted him to check everywhere, so he would.

And then he saw them: signs that an animal of some kind had been through here—definitely a large animal, one heavy enough, and broad enough, to have bruised and trampled the budding undergrowth.

"All righty, fella," he said to himself and to the nosy chipmunk watching him from a dead log off to his right, "we got . . . a big bear or . . . maybe," he pointed at it with his two index fingers as he spoke, "a big in-di-vidual. Whaddya think, bud?" The chipmunk shrugged and hopped off the log.

Broken branches on a young balsam crowding the area pulled him off to the right. It wasn't easy to see. Tall oak trees budding overhead cast shadows, and the slender arms of scrubby half-grown pines threatened to poke him in the eye. But someone had barged through here before him—that was obvious. Someone heavy enough to crush the ferns that were thrusting upward from their winter sleep.

He was fifty yards from the shack when his boots slipped on the soft hummocks of a small bog. Ray stopped and looked around. Someone else had stopped here, too. The brush ahead of him appeared untouched.

He studied the tag alders that had sprung up in the patches of sunlight exposing the bog. That's when he saw it: a golf club resting in tag alder branches less than ten feet from where he was standing. Had the previous visitor thought they could wing the golf club over the tag alders and into the bog? If so, they didn't get it quite that far. But what the hell? Rather than get their feet wet, whoever it was must have given up, knowing no human being in their right mind would ever find their way out here.

Ray reached for the camera he had slung over his shoulder. He preferred that to the camera on his phone. Better zoom, better light. He could work with it digitally and get great shots both for the photos he sold to the insurance agency for their annual calendar and the crime-scene photos he had shot for Chief Ferris. She insisted that his photos were better—clearer and better angled—than what she could get from the crime lab's photographer. Plus it took that guy an hour or more to get where she needed him. More than once Ray's photos had been instrumental in her investigations. Today could be one of those instances: thanks to the bog, it was easy to make out the deep patterns made from the boots of whoever had been here before. No doubt a couple of these shots could be useful.

Only after taking the photos did Ray throw the camera back over his shoulder and push through the tag alder to reach the golf club, a steel six-iron with a red stain on one end where it appeared to be broken. Pulling on the Laetrile gloves he had tucked into the pocket of his cargo pants, Ray grabbed the closest section of the broken club.

He was able to reach the other without slipping farther into the bog.

*   *   *

On the way out, Ray pulled into the drive at the McDonough house, where one of the Wausau boys was parked near the garage. After identifying himself and explaining what he had found and where, he asked the investigator if there happened to be a set of golf clubs in the house or the garage.

"Yes, in the far right corner of the garage," said the man, pointing. "You can't miss it. There's a set of shelves right beside it."

Ray walked over to take a look. Yes, the six-iron he had found at the bog matched the set here in Grace McDonough's garage. But Ray was no golfer. He'd better let someone else check that out.

As he drove home, he called in to the police department and got Marlaine on Dispatch, who said that Chief Ferris had not returned from the funeral yet. "Unless you're dying yourself, I wouldn't call her cell phone. You know what I mean, right?" said Marlaine. He left a message for Chief Ferris to call him ASAP when she returned.

Whistling, he pulled onto the dirt road leading down to his trailer home. Now he could think about that brilliant new podcast idea that had dawned on him early that morning: Why not target women? More and more women are interested in fishing, aren't they? And now he has the perfect student: Dr. Lisa Carter.

Yep, Ray was happy. He whistled all the way down to the giant fish that he had painted across the front of his trailer so that he—and all unsuspecting visitors—had to enter through its gaping jaws.

# Chapter Twenty-One

Arriving at Lew's office on the dot of four that afternoon, Lisa Carter had such a serious look on her face that Lew had to wonder what was wrong. She was dressed for business in a tailored dark-gray suit and low black heels. Her curly light-brown hair was tucked primly behind her ears, and light makeup had been applied with care. In spite of Lisa's worried expression, Lew couldn't help kidding her.

"Are you wearing that outfit fishing tonight?" she asked with a grin as she marshaled Lisa over to a chair at the low table in the corner of the room. Surprise that Lew knew of her plans crossed Lisa's face as she sat down under the picture window overlooking the newly green lawn and tall oak trees guarding the hundred-year-old courthouse.

Answering the question in Lisa's eyes, Lew said, "Ray told me you've booked him for a lesson with a spinning rod. So I'm kidding. I'm sure you'll change clothes before then. Do you need a place to change?"

"Thank you, but I'm staying over at the Loon Lake Inn so I won't have to rush through my lesson later," said Lisa matter-of-factly. "Not after paying what Mr. Pradt charges."

Lew kept her mouth shut. She didn't add that it never hurts to plan ahead and Lisa might want to spend a little time post-lesson with a particularly good-looking "Mr. Pradt."

Instead Lew said, "Thank you for driving up this afternoon. My brother's memorial service was earlier today and I apologize, as I haven't had time to look over the case reports you e-mailed this afternoon."

"You're welcome, Chief Ferris," said Lisa, "but don't apologize, please. I finished my reports minutes before leaving to drive up here so they haven't been in the system very long. Frankly, this meeting will be helpful, as I have some questions separate from the reports."

"Did Bruce Peters tell you Ray found a broken golf club that may have something to do with the investigation of Noah McDonough's death?"

"Yes, and that is very interesting. But if you don't mind, I'd like to start with my results from examining the first victim, Grace McDonough."

"Go right ahead."

"As I say in the case report, my results show the woman had been drinking heavily before she died. Her blood alcohol level was so high that had she been on the road in her car and stopped by law enforcement, they would have had to arrest her for drunk driving. But that couldn't happen because she was dead before she got in that car. Smothered."

"Smothered?" Lew was taken aback.

"Yes. Not strangled—smothered. With a pillow perhaps? A blanket or heavy clothing of some kind? I've alerted Bruce to have his investigative team test sofa and bed pillows from the house as well as any other items that could have been used to apply that kind of pressure.

"My theory—and it is just a theory at this point—is that the woman drank enough to doze off and someone took advantage of the moment. And because of something else I found, Chief, I believe her death was premeditated.

"On removing the clothing from the victim, I was struck by the condition of the body relative to the clothing. The woman had on a pair of blue jeans, but they had been buckled so loosely that if she were alive and stood up, the jeans would have fallen down. From the size and wear patterns I believe the jeans were her own, but I find it hard to believe she put them on herself."

"Are you're saying someone put the jeans on the body after death?"

"Yes. But no underwear. No underpants or panties and, as a woman who wears jeans often, I find that difficult to believe. What do you think?"

Lew looked at Lisa. "Was she raped?"

"No. No evidence of sexual assault. Not on the body, nor on the clothing. No question of rape."

"Then the missing underwear is very odd."

"There's more. My examination of Noah McDonough's body showed cause of death was a stab wound in the neck compounded by blunt trauma. He had been hit hard from behind across the neck region. When I removed the clothing from that victim, his hiking shorts had been shoved up quite high—again as if yanked onto the body after death."

Lisa's tone was matter-of-fact as she said, "That victim's underwear was also missing. Don't most men wear jockey shorts or boxers?" She tipped her head sideways as she said, "Again, what do you think? And I should add there is no question of a sexual assault having occurred in this case either."

"Depending on the hiking shorts, I would think going around with no underwear could be uncomfortable for most young men," said Lew. "What you're telling me is that both victims were missing their underwear." Lew sat quiet, thinking. "What about my brother's body?"

"He was fully clothed."

"So we have a weirdo on the loose."

"Appears that way. Here's the thing, Chief Ferris," said Lisa, "I'm familiar with people stealing women's underwear. For many reasons. For example, when I was in college there was a girl in our dorm who crept into our rooms and stole our underwear. Now that *was* weird. They sent her to a therapist." Lisa grimaced. "No idea what her problem was, but she did graduate."

"And she stopped stealing underwear?"

"Yes."

Lew leaned forward, her forearms on her knees, hands clasped together. "If I assume that the same person killed both mother and son," she said, "and we have no proof of that yet, but if I make that assumption, then it appears we may have a killer who collects trophies."

Lisa was silent. Finally she said, "That's disturbing."

"Three murders so close together in such a small community as Loon Lake is disturbing," said Lew.

"By the way, how big is Loon Lake?" asked Lisa. "Looks pretty small town to me."

"My jurisdiction covers the Loon Lake Township, which has a population of three thousand, two hundred and fifteen," said Lew. "McBride County, which we are part of, is thirty-five thousand, so we aren't that small. You might be surprised to learn that we draw over a hundred thousand tourists during the summer months, plus we just had the opening of the fishing season, and that drew thousands of people to the area.

"The Northwoods is popular with people from Chicago and Milwaukee, Minneapolis, Detroit—you name it. Even your old hometown Kansas City. It's not just the fishing they love but the hiking, the swimming, the bike trails, the bird watching, camping—summer camps for kids."

"Whoa, with that many people coming and going—where do you even start?"

"Good question," said Lew. "In my brother's case, I learned today that he had received threatening phone calls related to work he was involved in. He and a group of environmental activists have been planning to file a lawsuit protesting a sulfide mine project that could pollute one of our major rivers. So that, at least, gives me a starting point."

"I don't envy you your job," said Lisa as she handed several documents to Lew. "These are copies of my case reports on both victims and your brother. Save you from printing them out." She paused. "Is it okay to share this information with Ray Pradt?"

"Yes. Ray is a good friend and works for my department when I need an expert tracker on land or water. He's also an excellent photographer. Better, frankly, than some of the people your crime lab sends up here. So when I can afford it, I use him to shoot crime scenes."

She didn't mention that, thanks to his predilection for an agricultural product still illegal in Wisconsin, Ray was her best source for tapping into current events among the bad actors living down roads with no fire numbers. "He knows what to keep confidential."

Walking her to the door, Lew said, "You're leaving me with a lot to think about, Lisa. Good luck with your lesson on the water this evening. Fishing is the best way in the world to take your mind off troubles."

"I need that," said Lisa with a hopeful smile.

"I do too." Lew smiled back.

*     *     *

She was about to sit back down at her desk when her phone rang.

"Lewellyn," said the voice that always reached her heart. "Don't forget my place tonight."

"I haven't forgotten," said Lew, breathing a sigh of relief. She checked her watch. "Looks like I'll be there in an hour or so. I'm holding a brief press conference in twenty minutes and then that's it for my day. At least I hope that's it for the day."

"Good. Bring a pie." They both laughed.

It was a private joke. A month after Osborne's wife, Mary Lee, had died unexpectedly of a bronchial infection that turned deadly in the height of a paralyzing snowstorm, he became the target of a neighbor woman who was convinced they were perfect for each other. She wooed the new widower with pies—every few days

Osborne would find a delicious new pie left on his door-step. But life isn't just about pie. After a time, he had been able to discourage her without, he'd hoped, hurting her feelings.

Lew, on the other hand, had made one thing clear from the start of their relationship: no pies; she didn't bake. Tie trout flies? Yes. But apple, peach, and rhubarb pie? Sorry. He'd have to make his own.

\* \* \*

Relaxing on the sofa after enjoying Osborne's spaghetti made with some venison he'd shot last Thanksgiving, Lew mulled over the case reports from the forensic pathologist. "I mean, this is so bizarre, Doc," she said, after the third time she had repeated the details of Lisa Carter's discovery that both McDonoughs had been found missing their underwear.

Osborne sighed. "Lewellyn, let's sleep on it. No easy answers tonight and you know that."

"You're right. I'll shut up. But . . ."—she kept going even as Osborne rolled his eyes—"I wonder if I did the right thing not letting the reporters know about that during the press conference this afternoon. Maybe I should have said something, maybe that could trigger something that someone reading the paper or watching the news might bring to my attention."

"Not too late to hold another press conference tomorrow and say something new has come to your attention. But clarify one fact for me—Lisa Carter found nothing that might connect what happened to the McDonough family to Pete, right?"

"Well, I know the answer to that at least," said Lew, getting to her feet. She had changed into khaki shorts and a sweatshirt. "Normandy Mining LLC hired a hit man." She grimaced at her bad joke, and Osborne shook his head. "No, I don't see a connection to the McDonoughs, but on the other hand I don't see what happened to Pete as the result of a random act."

"That's enough for now," said Osborne. "C'mon, follow me down to the lake." He slid open the screen door leading to the porch and down to the dock. "Let's catch the sunset."

Just as late May could deliver two feet of snow, so could mid-May be an unseasonable eighty degrees in the early evening. Tonight was one of those nights. The sun was hovering over the pointed firs on the far side of the lake. Lew and Osborne sat silent, listening to the ripples lapping along the shore. A kingfisher swooped overhead, and an owl hooted somewhere far away.

A surprise drifted slowly into view from the right: a familiar Alumacraft or, as Ray liked to call his favorite fishing boat, "seventeen feet of heaven." With his hand Osborne signaled to Lew to say nothing, just watch. It was obvious the occupants of the boat were unaware they were being observed.

Two figures were on board: one sitting, arms crossed; the other standing to cast a spinning rod first to one side, then another. After several casts, the woman reeled in her line, held the rod up, and inspected the hook at the end. "Worm's gone, dammit," she said.

"Good. Someone had a nice meal," said a male voice. "You have to work harder on setting the hook. Okay, try another one."

The woman leaned down to reach into a small pail, then sat and, concentrating hard, tried to work the nightcrawler onto the hook. The worm squirmed out of her hand. "Dammit."

"Lisa, you deal with grim stuff every day," said her instructor. "You have to be able to hook a worm."

"Yeah, well, my subjects don't wriggle—yikes!" Another nightcrawler hit the deck.

"All right, let's start over. I'll show you again, so watch closely." Ray got up from his captain's chair to kneel beside Lisa, his instructions carrying easily across the water to where two spectators sat, delighted to be witnessing Lisa's dilemma and Ray's attempt at patience.

"First, hook the worm through the nose . . ."

"This damn thing has a nose?"

"Yes . . ."

"Okay, I think I see it. Got it."

"Now push the barb out the bottom like this . . . and rebury the hook dead center in the nightcrawler—see? Try not to have the hook point exposed . . . when you feel a bite . . . you want to make sure you strike hard enough to move the hook into the fish's mouth."

"Why do I have to do this with a damn worm?" asked Lisa. "Why can't I use one of those fancy lures you showed me before? One of those musky lures with all the hooks? They don't wriggle when you put 'em on."

"No," said Ray, his voice firm. "This lesson is not about the nightcrawler. I'm teaching you how to set a hook. You need the basics before you go high tech."

"Oh, for heaven's sake, I don't believe you. You're just having fun watching me struggle with these wriggling monsters."

Osborne cleared his throat. The two on the boat looked over. Ray waved. Lisa, surprised, stood up to wave hello, and toppled over the side of the boat.

"It's waist deep!" shouted Osborne as Lisa's head surfaced. "Don't worry. You can stand easily, then walk to the dock here and I'll help you up."

"Oh, gosh, I am so embarrassed," said Lisa, her hair, T-shirt, and shorts dripping as she pushed through the water. Trolling motor running, Ray steered his boat to the opposite side of the dock and stepped out onto the sandy shoreline. "Are you okay?" he asked his student.

All he got in return was a dirty look.

"Of course I'm okay," said Lisa, muttering as she accepted the beach towel Lew had grabbed for her. "Think I like fly-fishing better. No worms, dammit."

Once Lisa had stopped shivering, she and Ray sat down in the folding picnic chairs that Osborne had hurried to set out. "Oh, this feels good," said Lisa, relaxing into her chair and tucking the beach towel around her legs. "Guess I'm lucky this is such a warm evening."

"You're lucky to have a good instructor," said Osborne, "worms aside. Ray is one of the best fishing guides in the region."

"Doc's not saying that just to be nice," said Lew.

"He wants me to be on his podcast to try to entice other women to do battle with nightcrawlers," said Lisa with a laugh.

"You should," said Lew. "Then you and I will do one for women fly-fishing beginners. I'll have you demonstrate while I talk about the difference in how you cast a fly rod versus a spinning rod. Did you notice the difference, Lisa? How you move your arm away from the body when you cast a spinning rod?"

"Really? You'll do a podcast for women learning to fly-fish?" Ray sounded disheartened.

"N-o-o, I'm kidding," said Lew. "I would never think of poaching your audience, you know that." She winked at Lisa. Before Ray could say more, Lew asked, "Did Lisa tell you the unusual results of her autopsies?"

"Yes," said Ray, his face turning serious, "and I want to mention something about Grace McDonough."

Well aware that voices carry over water, Ray leaned forward and said in a low, quiet tone, "Back in my pre-AA days, I ran into Grace frequently during the summer. She hung out at the same bars, and you couldn't miss her—that husky cigarette voice and her loud laugh. She held court. And that woman could drink. I don't know how she made it home without taking out a tree or a mailbox or another car. Grace McDonough drank to get drunk. Being drunk and rich can make you a prime target for some razzbonya," he said, using the local vernacular for nincompoop.

"So the blood alcohol level doesn't surprise me. But one more thing, Chief. I made a few phone calls this afternoon, and she's been seen around the bars these last few weeks with a mutual friend of ours—Stan Mayer."

"That fits," said Osborne. "Steve Keran from First National Bank said that Stan is handling the sale of some of her land to Normandy Mining. Wonder what happens to that now?"

"Good question," said Ray. "Nothing I hope. Who the hell wants a sulfide mine alongside the Pelican River?

One thing for sure—that'll ruin Loon Lake's tourism business." The others nodded in agreement.

"So we know she hung out with Stan recently," said Lew. "Did they mention anyone else? I don't see Stan risking his found money since he's been brokering her real estate deal."

"No, but I'll keep asking around. Maybe stop in at one of the bars where she's been a regular. But what about the kid? Who did he hang with? Do we have any idea? I'll mention his name too. Wait." Ray paused. "I know. I'll check with a guy I know who deals dope. He may know."

"Could it be that Grace picked up someone and her son caught the person assaulting her?" asked Lisa.

"That's not a bad scenario," said Ray, thinking. "He walked in on some creep taking advantage of his mother when she was out of it and . . ."

"And things got out of hand." Doc finished Ray's thought.

"So you're in AA?" asked Lisa, "Sorry, but you brought it up."

"No problem," said Ray with an easy grin. "Three years sober, I'm proud to say."

"Me, too," said Osborne. "Ray and I go to meetings together."

"Oh . . ." Lisa was taken aback.

"Alcoholism is alleged to be Wisconsin's state sport," said Lew. "I don't mean that, of course, but plenty of us have had to deal with it in our families, our friendships, our professional lives."

"All right. This is too serious for a lovely summer evening," said Ray, putting an end to the discussion. "Lisa, if you'll trust my navigation skills, please climb back into the boat and we'll head around that white pine there and back to my place."

"More worm instruction I hope not?"

"Nope, you've graduated to a mud puppy."

"That's sounds as attractive as a worm."

"Hey, it's a surface lure, not a worm."

Lisa looked skeptical. "Oh, yeah? Mud puppy, huh. Can't wait."

\*   \*   \*

Watching as Ray pushed the boat off the shore and stepped into it, Lew recalled her second month as the new officer in the police department. She was on duty late one night when she got a call that someone had spotted a drunk driver on County Highway E heading east. Five minutes after receiving the call, she pulled the driver over. She recognized the man immediately. He was the recently retired dentist to whom she had taken her son and daughter for their grade-school exams. The dentist? Dr. Paul Osborne. Pre-AA Dr. Paul Osborne.

\*   \*   \*

Going up the stone steps to Osborne's well-lit porch, Lew stopped and turned back to look toward the rose-streaked sky that was slowly darkening. A full moon had emerged from the pines guarding the eastern shore, but it wasn't having an easy time as it tried to push through a scrim of dark-gray clouds. The moon would peek through for an instant only to be smothered by the ghostly blanket.

Reminding herself that she didn't believe in ghosts, Lew shivered as she started back up the stairs.

Ghosts? No. Omens? That was another story.

# Chapter
# Twenty-Two

Bruce was in her office by ten that Tuesday morning, his eyebrows hanging so low over his eyes that Lew knew he was perplexed. Bruce did not like to be perplexed. He liked to gather data, analyze results, and move on. This Tuesday morning did not look like a "move on" kind of day.

In less than a minute Lew found herself recovering from his opening statement: "The DNA from skin cells on the broken golf club used to stab Noah McDonough in the neck matches similar skin-cell DNA found on that pry bar used to kill your brother Pete."

Lew sat silent, waiting for him to say more. But he was quiet, eyebrows twitching with consternation.

"That's all we got so far. No matches in the law enforcement databases yet. Though we do have one match, which is Noah McDonough. His DNA from Dr. Carter's autopsy matches the DNA sample in California where he was booked last year on suspicion of enticing a minor.

"Chief, our search isn't over yet. With five point six million DNA samples from criminals and criminal suspects across the country, I've been hoping we'd get a match. Could be someone recently released from prison."

"But two such unrelated victims, Bruce. It's difficult to believe the DNA samples on the two weapons are a match. Doesn't make sense."

"No, it doesn't—until it does, Chief. But I'm working the puzzle. Right now I'm doing something our crime lab hasn't done before. Actually, we couldn't. GEDMatch has only been available for the last few years. But I've got that search going, so we'll see what we get."

"You lost me," said Lew. "What is GEDMatch?"

"It's a nonprofit research database where users can upload genetic data from ancestry tests like 23andMe, AncestryDNA, Family Tree DNA and My Heritage," said Bruce. "That is if people have agreed to allow law enforcement to use their DNA. And if they have, then GEDMatch allows us to search the DNA samples from different companies."

"I see. You may find someone who has never been arrested for a serious crime."

"Correct. I hope to have the results from both searches by the end of the day today. But I thought you should know about the DNA match to fingermarks on both the pry bar and the golf club. We're fortunate that we've had recent advances in DNA testing—our techs couldn't have done this a year ago."

"Please thank your colleagues for me," said Lew, "and let's keep this quiet until we know more."

"Of course."

"Anything new on the Grace McDonough case?" she asked. "I know Dr. Carter has determined the woman was dead before her body was put in the car—"

"No, my team is working the house again—the pillows, bed covers, bath towels, kitchen towels, clothing. If the woman was smothered in her home or in her car, we'll find how and where. We will, I'm sure we will."

Bruce looked so grim that Lew knew he was worried. He got to his feet, closed the file he had brought in with him and headed for the door, then paused. "Are you doing okay, Chief?" The brows had changed shape to express his concern for her. "Not easy losing a sibling. Happened to me years ago when I was kid. My older brother was killed in a hit-and-run. He was fourteen and on the new bike my folks had just given him for his birthday."

The brows closed in on themselves. "That's why I went into this . . . line of work." His voice cracked and he rushed out the door before Lew could invite him to fish the Prairie with her that weekend.

\* \* \*

Sitting at her desk, the room quiet, Lew mulled over her campaign for sheriff. Did she really want to take on the responsibility of fifty-plus deputies and all the administrative issues the position would bring?

More important was how closely she now worked with people like Bruce Peters, like Ray Pradt and Dani Wright, like Doc—even Lisa Carter, whom she didn't know that well but liked. She would lose the closeness of working with people who were more than colleagues. "They're my friends," she thought.

A soft knock on the door to her office interrupted her thoughts. "Come in."

"Lew?" It was Charlotte Mayer. "Do you have a few minutes? I've been thinking hard about something that I probably shouldn't share. But the more I worry over it, the more I think maybe I should."

"Come in and sit down," said Lew. Charlotte's public health office was in a separate wing of the old courthouse, so it was easy for her to drop in. Though they saw each other at the city council meetings monthly, since Melanie's death Charlotte had not been a frequent visitor. Given that it was only a day since their chat before Linda's peculiar memorial service for Pete, this was unusual. "I . . . well . . . I have to tell you something that is really is none of my business."

"Go ahead. If it has to stay confidential, my lips are sealed." Lew gave her an encouraging smile. *Please don't tell me you're moving back in with that colossally stupid ex-husband of yours*, she prayed.

"It's Stan," said Charlotte. She paused, and Lew hoped against hope.

"He's been having an affair with Linda—Pete's Linda. I know it's not important but I wanted—"

"I know all about it," said Lew, raising a hand.

"You do?" Charlotte was taken aback. "I thought just me and Johnny . . ."

"Pete told Bridget. He was planning to file for divorce. May have in fact. I'm not sure."

"Whew," said Charlotte. "I didn't want to be delivering bad news, but I don't like that woman and I'm not sure she'll be fair to Bridget. How is Bridget by the way?"

"She's been staying with me, though she had to go back to school yesterday morning. She'll be back Friday and we'll work together on taking care of things. Yeah, Linda's a piece of work. All I can say is my poor brother was so damn lost after Melanie died that he didn't know what he was doing."

"If it makes you feel any better, she'll get what she deserves with Stan. I kick myself to this day for marrying the guy just because he was the first one I—"

"I know, I know," said Lew holding up one hand and shaking her head. "You're not the only one who made that mistake." The two women rolled their eyes as they commiserated over their mutual marital blunders.

"Stan is such a miserable individual, and I say that because of what he's doing to our son."

"Oh?" Lew sat up straight. She didn't want to hear that Stan was an abusive father.

"Little stuff," said Charlotte, "and I don't want you to waste your time listening to this." She started to get up from her chair, but Lew waved her down.

"Tell me. John is one of Mason's best friends, so both Doc and I need to know if there's anything we can do to help. Your son's a good kid."

Charlotte laughed, saying, "He'd like to hear you say that." Her expression turned serious. "My Johnny is a worrier. He worries about the dog, he worries if the birds have enough birdseed in our birdfeeder, he worries that other kids are being bullied . . . and he's very worried you might still arrest him for that citizen's arrest stunt."

Lew started to protest, but before she could Charlotte said, "I know, I know—I keep reassuring him that if he attends the sessions Erin has organized he'll be fine. It's this business with Stan that has me determined to get full custody of John." Charlotte gave Lew a nervous look. "We have a hearing next week, and I am so damn mad . . ."

"That bad?" asked Lew.

"It is and it isn't. Stan just . . . he neglects Johnny. He rarely does anything with him. God forbid he take him fishing or to throw a baseball. He skips the soccer practice and, worst of all, when Johnny stays over at his place,

Stan leaves him alone all night. Or almost all night. I know my son is twelve and old enough to be on his own, but he is a worrier. When he finds out his dad has left the house late at night, he worries. I know because he calls me to see if there's been an accident."

"Stan has John over how many nights a week?" asked Lew.

"It's supposed to be four nights with me, three with his dad, and every other weekend—joint custody. But when Johnny is at his place for the weekend, Stan's gone most of time. Says he's working, and maybe he is. If that's the case, then why not let John hang out in his office? All he needs is to be around his dad. But it's the nights that are scary for my son. Stan is renting a house on that road way back behind the old landfill. His neighbors are an empty barn and that bar that burned down a couple years ago. Johnny told me his dad leaves right after they eat lunch on Saturday and doesn't show up until late at night. Half the time he leaves a pizza at the house for Johnny to have for dinner. I know what he's doing—he's seeing that damn Linda out at our old cottage. At least that's what I think."

"And where's the cottage, Charlotte?"

"Out on Sand Lake. He got it in our divorce. It needs so much work I didn't care, plus I don't like that lake. Too many summer homes built right on top of each other. Now, Lew, I don't know for sure, but I think that's what he's up to. This has been going on for months now."

"I'm so sorry to hear this. Do you think you have a chance at full custody? That could be so settling for your son."

"I know. I'm hoping. I've had Johnny write down the dates for every time his dad is gone. The hours too. That might help."

"You're sure this has involved Linda all this time? I mean, she and Pete were only married for three years." Lew thought about that for a minute, then went on: "You know, Pete has always been happy to fill his weekends with projects. He used to enjoy woodworking, but recently it's been time spent with Loon Rescue and his work against the sulfide mine. He definitely left a door open for Linda to amuse herself. I'm sure she had an excuse too, like playing bridge with her girlfriends. Has your son seen Stan with Linda, or are we speculating?"

Charlotte lowered her voice as if she thought Lew's office was full of listening devices and said, "I shouldn't tell you this, but Johnny sneaks looks at his dad's cell phone, so he knows it's Linda who calls."

# Chapter Twenty-Three

Osborne was staring at the bottom of his empty coffee mug. Should he order a third and hang out with Herm and Ray for another fifteen or twenty minutes? His other McDonald's compatriots had already left, their Wednesday morning schedules calling them elsewhere.

"What are you up to later today?" Herm was asking Ray, when a familiar figure loomed over their table.

"Do not leave," said Steve Keron in his best banker-authority voice. "I have news you won't believe, but I need a cup of coffee first."

Eyebrows rose, no one moved.

Osborne suspected that, like him, the other two guys had nothing pressing to do, so a little gossip would be appreciated.

"A real game-changer happened this morning," said Steve as he sat down and leaned forward to keep his voice low. "I know I shouldn't be telling you, but I'm so close to retirement I can't be fired. Plus," he closed his eyes before adding, "this is so hard to believe that I have to tell someone—but keep it quiet, okay?"

Everyone nodded yes.

"Stan Mayer walked into the bank five minutes after we opened our doors. No appointment. Demanded to see the officer handling the McDonough trust . . ." Steve paused dramatically.

When he said nothing for a long minute, Osborne took the bait, "That would be you, right?"

"That would be me." A grin of satisfaction stole across the banker's face. "That would indeed be me." Again the pause.

Now Ray spoke up, "Hey, bud, I got half a dozen bluegills waiting . . ."

"He, uh, claims he is the heir to the McDonough trust—all the money, all the land."

The table was so silent it was as if the air had gone out of the room.

Finally the elder of the group spoke: "Do I hear you correctly that Stan, 'your expert real-estate appraiser' Mayer, alleges he is the heir to the California McDonough millions? Is that what I hear you saying?"

It was Herm, phlegmatic Herm, who had posed these questions. "You best tell us more, Mr. Keran."

"Not much more to tell, except he may be right."

"Whoa, wait a minute—" Ray stammered.

"Don't you have to have some kind of proof that you're family for that to happen?" asked Osborne.

Leaning back in his chair, Steve pointed an index finger at Osborne. "Correct. And he has that proof."

"A birth certificate with Old Man McDonough's sworn testimony that he and only he had an illicit relationship with the late Gloria Bertrand Mayer in spite of her supposed married name?" asked Osborne. "If that were true, wouldn't it have surfaced a long time ago?"

"He has something better than that," said Steve. "He has irrefutable proof from a geneticist with the Holder Clinic. Turns out she has a side venture in genealogy. She calls herself a 'family detective.' She tracked Stan's DNA, and it proves that he is a biological brother to the late Grace McDonough. Quite amazing and irrefutable, I think. The DNA match is fifty percent!"

"But he isn't named in Old Man McDonough's will, is he?"

"No. But there's nothing in the will to say that he cannot be named an heir. If he can prove his family connection through DNA, then he is a legitimate heir."

"No," Osborne persisted. "I find that very hard to believe."

"Doc, we've checked it out and the man is legit. He came in today because he wanted the bank as trustee of the McDonough estate to know that he has the right to complete the sale of Grace's land along the Pelican River to the Normandy Mining operation. I believe that sale goes through this coming Monday, although Stan told me he's still negotiating. They've offered thirty-five mil, but he said he's going to push for more. I told him not to be stupid, that thirty-five million is more than a parcel of land has ever sold for in the entire Northwoods. As the bank's executive handling the McDonough Trust, I'll likely be signing the papers for that sale Monday afternoon. Or, to put it another way," said Steve with a smirk, "I'll be signing a paper that will make our friend a multimillionaire."

He paused. Then, grinning widely, he said: "He'll be able to pay off the car loan on that miserable beat-up Honda he's been driving. Have you ever looked at that car? The left rear fender has a huge dent and the tires are flat-out bald. Vehicle has to be ten years old."

Conversation buzzed among the four men for another five minutes before Osborne had a thought. "Steve," he said, "do you mind telling me the name of the geneticist who has done the research on this? My oldest daughter is deep into genealogy and I know she would love to know about a 'family detective.'"

"Sure," said Steve. "Walk over to my office with me and I'll give you the woman's name and how to reach her. We're following up too, as we have to make sure all the legal issues are handled correctly."

The two men ducked out of the McDonald's just as rain clouds opened up. They dashed down the street to the entrance to the First National Bank. Once inside, Steve ushered Osborne into his office, which was in the front of the building, and opened one of several files sitting in the middle of his desk. He jotted down a name and number and handed the note to Osborne.

Osborne glanced down at the note and said, "You're sure it's okay to give me this? I'm not asking you for confidential information, am I?"

Steve chuckled. "Hardly. Stan told me he's so pleased that he's planning to hold a press conference the minute the Normandy Mining papers are signed. He wants the world to know who he is." The two men shook their heads.

Outside the bank and standing in the light rain, Osborne pulled out his cell phone. "Lew," he said, "I'm on my way over with a bombshell that will change your day." He gave her a quick sketch of what he had just learned. "You might want to ask Dani to join us. I'll bet a quick online search will tell us if this so-called family detective is legitimate."

"Got it," said Lew. "Did you say she works out of the Holder Clinic?"

"Yes."

"Cancel whatever you were planning to do today. The main offices of the Holder Clinic are in Wausau, and I'd like you to join me as I drop in on this individual. Do you mind? You're my health expert, Doc."

Osborne ran through the rain to his car and sped over to park at the Loon Lake police department. Lew and Dani were waiting for him.

"I've checked the clinic roster and confirmed that the genetic counselor Mr. Mayer would have seen is Kathryn Taylor," said Dani. "I then did another search and found that she has a side business called The Family Detective, where she teaches people how to do genealogical searches, or—for quite a bit of money—she will do it for you. She is also certified to work with law enforcement. Want to see her website?"

# Chapter
# Twenty-Four

Two hours later, Lew and Doc found themselves being welcomed into a spacious office at the Holder Clinic. The woman inviting them in with a broad smile was Kathryn Taylor, the clinic's genetic counselor, a tall, broad-shouldered woman with full cheeks that shook when she spoke and who seemed very pleased, if not excited, to see them.

"I checked Mr. Mayer's file before I told the bank I would agree to meet with you," she said with an air of authority. "I had to be sure that he would allow me to share his genetic information and"—she looked down at the file—"and he has, indeed, signed our Release of Information Authorization." She held up a form as she spoke.

"Usually, in a case like this—though I don't see many quite like this," she chuckled, "it's a lawyer who stops in, but I know you folks up north have your own way of doing things, don't you."

It wasn't a question. As she talked, Lew realized that the woman assumed she and Osborne had been sent by the First National Bank's trust department. She considered correcting that impression but quickly decided against it. If she was violating some law, she would deal with it later. Right now she needed everything there was to know about Stanley Mayer and his DNA.

After introducing herself, Lew beckoned toward Doc as she said, "Dr. Osborne is one of my associates and an expert in dental forensics."

"Really," said Kathryn, her smile growing wider. "You must find this fascinating, Dr. Osborne. I have done some work with dentists here in Wausau. In fact, we're putting together an online seminar on new developments in the field of DNA research and various aspects of dentistry. There is a lot happening with tooth pulp."

"Really? That sounds very interesting," said Osborne, hitching his chair forward as he spoke. "I'll be sure to leave you my contact information, as I'm active with the Wisconsin Dental Society and I'm sure many of my colleagues will be interested as well."

"You think so? I'm planning to leave my position here at the clinic to focus on my new business, Your Family Detective. My business plan is to combine the latest in DNA research with developments in genealogy. The combination of both sciences is yielding some amazing results."

"Sounds like an excellent business model," said Osborne, prompting an even wider smile from the woman. Lew made a mental note to give him her annual Best Bullshit Artist Award.

"Sorry to interrupt," said Lew, "but could we start at the beginning? How exactly did Mr. Mayer find you?"

"Good question," said Kathryn, waving an authoritative finger at her. "Especially given the wonderful twist that surprised the heck out of both of us."

She shook her head in amazement as she said, "Who knew that a simple DNA search—well, not so simple really, and I'll show you why that is—who knew that we would discover that he could be an heir to a modest fortune? Modest by his standards anyway. I know he's a very successful businessman but still . . . a hundred thousand dollars is a good deal of money in my world."

"Oh, for heaven's sake, in my world too," said Lew.

Osborne supported Kathryn's enthusiasm with an eager nod.

"So, yes. Where do I start?" said Kathryn, shuffling the papers in front of her. "Here it is. Lynch Syndrome is what brought Mr. Mayer into my office just seven months ago."

Noting the puzzled look on her guests' faces, she explained, "Lynch Syndrome is a marker in your DNA that can indicate you are at risk of developing colon cancer. Mr. Mayer had been experiencing digestive issues, and a colonoscopy led to his primary physician recommending he have his genetic profile done.

"Now," she gazed at Osborne and Lew, "you know what a friendly, smart man Mr. Mayer is, right?" They nodded, smiling, and not mentioning that some people, the two of them included, considered Stan a blowhard. Or, as Osborne's McDonald's buddies, those experts on human nature, liked to say when they spotted Stan in the chain's food line, "There goes Stan the Man—all talk, no action."

It didn't help that Stanley Mayer was not bad looking so he often had recently divorced women, especially women who were new in town, hanging around him until they knew better. This infuriated the bright but average-looking guys at Osborne's table.

"Well, Stanley and I got to talking," said Kathryn, "and I told him about my new venture in genealogy, so when he got a call out of the blue from a stranger who claimed they were biological siblings, I was the first person he called.

"He was very concerned, knowing that he has a reputation as a well-heeled businessman, that the caller, a woman, might be an imposter after his money."

"Of course. A natural assumption," said Lew. "Do you happen to know how this individual found him?"

"Yes. That's why my work was so critical to what is happening now." Kathryn's entire body appeared to inflate with pride as she spoke. "So when he called, he said that her bank had just notified him that she had left him an inheritance, and that surprised the dickens out of him."

"He said her bank had notified him. Is that correct?" asked Lew.

"Yes, why?" asked Kathryn, taken aback by the question.

Lew waved a dismissive hand, "No reason. Just confirming that the bank had notified him. Checking connections is all."

"Yes—

"Excuse me," said Osborne, "did you find that Mr. Mayer does or does not have Lynch Syndrome?"

Relieved to have the focus of the conversation back on her expertise, Kathryn said, "No, he does not, which was a huge relief."

"I can imagine," said Lew, encouraging Kathryn to continue.

"So—to back up a bit—when he first called to tell me this total stranger was alleging that she was his biological sister, I told Mr. Mayer we would need her DNA in order to confirm that. At that time, he said he had agreed to meet up with her in two weeks. She had invited him to a picnic at her summer cottage on Memorial Day and he . . . well . . . he was a little hesitant. Wouldn't you be?"

It was a rhetorical question. "Of course," said Lew, urging her to go on.

"What happened next was that sometime last week—days before he was going to meet her for the first time—he got the incredibly sad news that she had passed away unexpectedly."

Kathryn's eyes searched theirs as she said, "Stanley was stunned. I mean, how does that happen?" Lew noticed she had begun to speak of her client differently: now he was "Stanley," a friend.

"She died?" asked Osborne, disbelief in his voice.

"Yes," said Kathryn, continuing, "it was a brain aneurysm. Totally unexpected. The woman had no history of brain issues. Died in her sleep, and she was only in her forties." Kathryn raised her eyebrows to underscore the unusually early death.

"Her bank informed Stanley that he was listed as her only heir and was likely to receive one hundred thousand dollars from her estate. They also told him she had left a small amount to a homeless shelter in the region where she lived. That's when Stanley decided that, if we could confirm their familial relationship, he would make a significant contribution in her name. He wants her to be remembered. But now we had a problem. How could Stanley confirm their biological connection if she was dead? And that's where I could help. I told him to reach out to the funeral director in charge of the funeral arrangements for assistance."

"That makes sense," said Osborne. "But not that many people know you can get DNA from a deceased person outside of an autopsy. How fortunate that Mr. Mayer knows you."

"Yes," said Kathryn. "We were both fortunate, because that is the kind of work that will underscore the value of my new business. So Stanley followed up with the funeral director, and we have been able to confirm that Stanley and the woman are—I mean were— biological siblings."

Lew shook her head, apparently confused. "I'm amazed you could do that. What is the process exactly?"

"Well," said Kathryn, straightening her shoulders with pride, "it was pretty simple really. Stanley came to my office late last week with DNA samples from the funeral home and I put them through our system. He had two samples, but one was enough.

"First, he had the funeral director work with Dacron swabs, which are used in the medical profession for DNA collection. Stanley's swab samples were viable, as the funeral director had acted immediately on receiving the deceased's remains. As you might imagine, timing is critical to getting good samples. Stanley also had a piece of fabric cut from the clothing the deceased was wearing at the time of her death."

Kathryn grimaced slightly. "We were worried because it was from her underwear, but the funeral director told Stanley it might have skin cells that could work if the swabs didn't. As it turned out, we didn't need to use that." She gave a look of relief.

"This is fascinating," said Osborne. "What did you do next?"

"Yes, that is when my work really began," said Kathryn. "I took the woman's DNA and began a search to see if we might have a match with Stanley's.

"I went to GEDMatch, a research database that has data from all the ancestry tests like 23andMe, Ancestry/DNA, Family Tree DNA and My Heritage. GED-Match allows people to search tests from all those sources as long as the individual has given permission to allow the searches, including those by law enforcement—and most people do. And that is where we found Stanley's match with his biological sister, a woman named Grace!"

Kathryn sat back with triumph on her face. "Can you believe it?"

"A heartwarming story," said Osborne.

"Yes," said Lew. "But Mr. Mayer had to put his DNA into the data search too, correct?"

"Yes. He certainly did, which is why we could make it work."

"I wonder when he did that? I mean, put his DNA into one of the search databases . . ." Lew made sure to sound offhand.

"I have no idea," said Kathryn, "but the fact is, he was there and we made this wonderful discovery."

"Well," said Lew, getting to her feet and extending a hand to Kathryn. "I can't thank you enough for spending this time with us."

"My pleasure," said Kathryn as she reached into her desk drawer. "And here are my cards for the new business. Please keep me in mind." She handed the cards over. Lew noticed she gave Osborne more than one.

\* \* \*

Lew and Osborne left the building and ran for Lew's cruiser. The rain that had been steady earlier was coming down even harder, leaving large puddles in the clinic parking lot.

"Stan Mayer is one lucky guy," said Lew, climbing into the cruiser. "Since the Wausau media can't be bothered to cover what happens in small town, boring Loon Lake, our 'family detective' hasn't heard that a Grace McDonough died recently, and not of a brain aneurysm. Thank goodness I've kept the autopsy results under wraps from the press."

As she buckled her seat belt, Lew added, "I wonder what that woman will think when she finds out that every word she heard from Stan Mayer—including 'a' and 'the'—was a lie."

# Chapter
# Twenty-Five

❧

Five houses down from Osborne's home on Loon Lake Road, Margie Caldwell sat at her kitchen table mulling over a phone call she wanted to make—or didn't want to make.

"Oh, go ahead," she told herself. "it works or it doesn't work. If it doesn't work, so what—you can still get to go to the party."

Bolstering herself with that thought, she picked up her cell phone and punched in the number that she read on the list of names attached to the invitation to her twentieth high school reunion.

* * *

Stan Mayer's name had jumped out the minute she saw the list. Oh, gosh, how long had it been? Twenty years? Twenty years, one marriage and one divorce ago?

She had pulled out her yearbook and studied the photo of the boy she had once hoped would invite her to the Junior Prom. He was cute and tall, and all her girl-friends had been sure he would choose her. But he didn't. Instead, like three other boys in her class, he had invited tiny, chirpy, totally irritating Mary Oberman. As Stan was first in line, he got Mary. Mary, who was now tiny, chubby, and just as irritatingly chirpy as she had been twenty years ago. Margie couldn't really be sure about that for she hadn't seen the woman since their gradua-tion, but she was positive it had to be the case.

The list of names was partnered with color photos of everyone who had RSVP'd for the reunion, so Margie was able to get a good look at forty-year-old Stan. Not bad. A little fuller in the face maybe, and he wore glasses now. But he looked a heck of a lot better than a lot of men his age. And, in her humble opinion, Margie knew she looked better than many of her former classmates. The good news was that irritating Mary Oberman wasn't on the list, so she must not be coming to the reunion.

Margie saw that, like her, Stan was divorced. He described himself as "an entrepreneurial real-estate inves-tor," which made him sound like a man who had made a few bucks. "Hmm," thought Margie. "This is all looking so good I need to get over my butterflies and just pick up the damn phone."

And so she had.

\* \* \*

Stan answered on the second ring. "Margie?"

"How'd you know it was me?" Margie was dumbfounded.

"Your name came up on my phone."

"Of course, silly me." Margie heard herself laugh a little too nervously. She tried to recover, "Yes, it's me, Stan. I'm in town for the reunion. Are you going to the get-together tomorrow night?"

Silence, and Margie started to curse herself. This was not a good idea after all.

"Sorry," said Stan after a long pause. "I needed to get to the other room so I could have some privacy. No, Margie, I forgot all about the reunion. But it's Friday, right?"

"With an early get-together tomorrow at the Loon Lake Pub. I'm just checking in with a few old friends to see if they're going, and I thought of you. I was remembering when we shared that desk in Geometry."

Stan chuckled. "Yeah, I remember that. Thank you again for letting me see your answers on the final. Saved my ass, girl."

"Well, okay, just wanted to say 'boo' and hope to catch up with you Friday." Margie was working on making a gracious exit.

"No, wait, are you going tomorrow?"

"Sure am. I kept my parents' home here so I visit once or twice a year and, yeah, I'm planning on it. Be fun to see people."

"Sure will. Could I pick you up?"

Margie did her best to sound nonchalant. "Well, that would be nice. Thank you. Look for you around . . . five or so? The get-together is for cocktails."

"Then let's do dinner after if you're up for it."

"Sounds great, Stan. You remember my folks' address?"

"Sure do. Didn't we go out once or twice our sophomore year?"

"Same place. Look for you then."

"Oh, and one thing, Margie. I'll be driving a crummy old Honda SUV. Hope you don't mind. My Range Rover is in the shop, and they gave me a real beater to drive."

"Heavens, no big deal," said Margie, her voice brimming with happiness. "See you then, Stan."

She hung up. And danced around the kitchen. It wasn't the prom, but this might be even better. Time to think about what to wear.

# Chapter
# Twenty-Six

❧

They were five miles from town when Lew's personal cell phone rang.

"Hi, Dani, whatever you're calling about, can it wait? I should be at the station in less than fifteen minutes."

"Good. I'm calling to be sure you come to the station ASAP, Chief. Something has happened. I'll be waiting for you."

"What—" Lew could hear guarded excitement in her voice. "Tell me."

"No, you have to see it. Doesn't make sense unless you see it. We're waiting . . ." And the phone clicked off.

"What's that all about?" asked Osborne.

"I'm not sure," said Lew, "You heard what I heard— Dani said something has happened. Sounds like something big, but she wouldn't say more." She stepped on the gas. "Dammit, I don't want to drive too fast in this downpour but . . ."

"Dani is sharp," said Osborne, "and she knows you. If she says, 'you have to see it' then you have to see it. I was going to have you drop me at my car but, if you don't mind, I'd like to see what this is about."

"After what we learned this afternoon, that makes two of us."

Lew managed to pull into her parking spot in less than ten minutes. With Osborne right behind her, she nodded to Marlaine at the front desk and hurried down the hall to Dani's cubicle.

Dani looked up from her desk, her eyes serious. The room was silent, so silent Lew could hear the rain drumming against the windows. Dani's eyes shifted toward another person in the room, Charlotte. Lew had never seen her friend looking so stricken.

"Charlotte? What are you doing here?" asked Lew.

"I was on my way home when I decided to stop by your office for a minute. You weren't there, so I was going to ask Dani to give you a message."

Before Charlotte could say more, Dani motioned for Lew to look at her computer screen. "I was going back over that footage we got from the trail cameras when Charlotte walked in looking for you, Chief."

"Yes," said Charlotte, "I was going to see if you had plans for dinner this evening—but when I peeked over Dani's shoulder, I . . ." Talking so fast she stumbled over her words, Charlotte said, "I couldn't . . . I could not believe what I saw." As she spoke and pointed to the screen, Charlotte's hand shook; her entire body seemed to vibrate.

Lew leaned forward to study the screen. Images from the Loon Rescue cameras that had been set farther back from the loon nest were flashing by; the images that showed Pete walking down the slight incline toward the loons were followed, seconds later, by those of a dark figure—a tall, thick-set figure moving in the same direction as Pete but visible only from the back.

"That's Stan." Charlotte's voice shook. "I'd know him anywhere. Goddammit, Lew, that's Stan! I know that shape, that walk, that hunch in the shoulders. I know the windbreaker." Charlotte grabbed Lew's arm saying, "You have got to arrest him. Now. He's supposed to pick my son up in an hour. I can't let that happen." She was hysterical.

Lew pulled her over to a chair. "You're sure that's Stan?" The fury in Charlotte's eyes made it seem as if she'd slug Lew if she didn't believe her. "All right. I got it. Calm down—take a deep breath. Don't worry, we'll get John and keep him safe until I can arrange a warrant for Stan's arrest"

"I am so sure, Lewellyn. I will testify in court."

"Okay," said Lew. "But first I need you to calm down. I believe you, Charlotte. But I do need more. That series of images does not show a face, and an angry ex-wife is not a valid witness. So, calm down while we work this out, okay?"

Lew looked over at Doc, who had been watching. "Do you know where Stan's office is?" She checked her watch. "I wonder if he might be there this late?"

"It's only four-thirty," said Osborne. "His office is over the music store on Stevens Street and next door to the Emory Law Firm."

"What's the name of his business?" asked Lew, pulling out her cell phone.

"Mayer Appraisals," said Charlotte, breathing easier.

Lew punched in the number that came up on her phone and waited. "Hello, Stan? Good afternoon. This is Chief Ferris. Say, I need to stop by and ask you a few questions regarding your work on the McDonough property. Can I see you in, oh, fifteen minutes?" She made sure she sounded genial. "Good, thank you."

What Lew didn't tell Stan was that after meeting with Kathryn Taylor she was determined to get what federal law required in order to arrest a suspect: a fresh sample of his DNA obtained with his permission.

Lew stared into the eyes of the three people watching her. "Why would he want my brother dead?"

"To protect the value of that property along the Pelican," said Osborne, "now that he can prove he is the rightful heir to the McDonough estate. That's why he appraised it so high."

"Doc's right," said Charlotte. "He knew that Pete's work against the sulfide mine was jeopardizing that deal. He's bragged to Johnny that he'll be making millions for his work on that land."

"But Rich Hartman has been working on that lawsuit too." Concern crossed Lew's face. "I better call Rich before I go over to Stan's office."

Hartman answered on the second ring.

"Rich, Chief Ferris here." No geniality in Lew's voice this time. "I can't tell you more at the moment, but I have good reason to believe you and your family may be in danger. I'm arranging for my officers, Todd Donovan and Roger Adamczak, to keep a watch on your home and neighborhood for the next forty-eight hours. You know Todd and Roger, so don't be alarmed when you see their squad cars. And, Rich, please talk to your family and see that everyone stays inside until I tell you it's safe."

"Is this about the lawsuit?"

"Tell you more when I can."

"I hear you," said Rich. "I haven't been aware of being followed, but something strange has happened. I went over to Pete's house this morning to get his file, a large brown envelope with the documentation for our lawsuit—"

Lew tried to get a word in.

"But it's not there, and that makes filing our lawsuit difficult. I'll have to contact his sources and hope I can get the documentation back in order in time to file before the McDonough sale goes through."

She tried again.

"Damn it all, we should have made copies. And now you're telling me I'm in danger? Hell, my case against Normandy Mining has evaporated too, goddammit."

"Rich, will you shut the hell up! Bridget has the envelope with those files. She's been planning to get it to you. Don't worry about that, okay?"

Lew checked her watch and started for the door saying, "Rich, just do what I say. Please? As soon as I know more, I'll call you."

"Yes, of course. I understand."

Osborne started to follow Lew but she stopped him. "No, Doc, I'll do this on my own." Osborne opened his mouth to protest. "No," Lew raised her right hand to stop him. "Don't worry, everything will be fine. Charlotte, is your son at your home right now?"

"Yes, until six."

"Tell him you forgot that Doc had planned a little party to surprise Mason for getting good grades and he's taking everyone out for pizza. I'll let Stan know there's been a change in plans."

"I'm on my way," said Charlotte.

"Lewellyn, be careful," said Osborne following Lew down the hall. "Be very, very careful."

Lew nodded. Osborne did not look reassured.

\* \* \*

She was dashing through the rain to her cruiser when her cell phone rang: Bruce. Climbing behind the wheel, she said, "Bruce, can this wait? I'm in a rush."

"Sure, Chief. Just giving you a heads-up that one of my investigators found a woman's sweatshirt, brand-new with the tags on it, crammed down into the recycle bin in the McDonough's garage. She thought it was odd to throw away a new shirt. If it is the shirt used to smother Grace McDonough, we may be able to get skin cells that'll match the killer's DNA. She's driving it down to the crime lab right now."

"Has she left yet?"

"Don't think so, why?"

"If you can catch her, I'll have a DNA sample I'd like her to take, too. Picking it up now."

"I'll try to reach her. If I can't, I'll let you know."

By the time Bruce hung up, Lew was pulling into a parking space in front of the building where Stan's office was on the second floor. She ran up the narrow stairway and knocked on the door marked Mayer Appraisals. Before Stan could answer, she let herself in.

"Hi there," she said, trying to smile.

He was getting up from behind an old oak desk as she walked toward him. "Well, this is unexpected. Hello, Chief Ferris, how can I help you?"

"I need a DNA sample from you, Stan," said Lew, holding out the plastic tube into which she wanted him to spit.

"What? Why?" Fear flashed in his eyes.

"One more step in our investigation of Grace McDonough's death."

"But that was an accident."

"It may be, but we haven't completed our investigation, which is required when someone dies under unusual circumstances. The Feds require us to check and see if someone else may have been in her car, so I'm gathering DNA samples from everyone who had been around Grace during the two weeks before her death." Lew kept her voice matter-of-fact. "You were handling business for her so I need a sample from you."

"Oh, I see." She could see Stan relax as he walked around the desk toward her. He took the tube, turned slightly, and spat. "Think that's good enough?"

"Should be. Thank you, Stan."

"Better check the bartender out at the Twelve Point Bar. She spent way too much time around that sonofabitch."

"Good tip, thanks. Oh, and I ran into Charlotte, who asked me to pass along that she forgot to tell you Johnny was invited to a party tonight. Mason's grandfather is taking a bunch of the kids for pizza because she got an A on her science test.

Stan, looking relieved, acknowledged the news with a nod. "Okay, thanks."

\* \* \*

Running down the stairs a minute later, Lew could imagine what Stan Mayer must be thinking: he had not been in Grace's car except on rare occasions, and he was sure to have worn gloves when putting her body into the Range Rover.

He would also assume that Lew must be getting DNA samples from people like Grace's banker, maybe several of the Normandy Mining guys who'd stopped by to meet with her, plus her drinking buddies. Yep, Stan had to figure he was one of many people who had spent time with Grace McDonough. Hardly a "person of interest."

"Bruce," said Lew on her cell phone as she climbed into her cruiser to return to the station, "where's your investigator? I've got this DNA sample from a person of interest in the murders of my brother and Noah McDonough, and as your lab has better technology than ours—"

"She's waiting for you at the station, Chief. Hey, any chance you'd be up for a day in the stream this next weekend?"

Lew exhaled. "Not sure. Let me get through tomorrow and I'll know." Then she gave him a brief description of what she had learned from Charlotte's response to the trail camera video and from the genetic counselor at the Holder Clinic.

Bruce was quiet when she had finished. "I'm calling Lisa Carter ASAP," he said. "We should be able to check the DNA sample against what we got from the golf club and the pry bar used on your brother and Noah McDonough. Call you in the morning."

"Or in the middle of the night," said Lew. "I'm going to have a hard time sleeping."

# Chapter
# Twenty-Seven

❧

Knowing sleep would be difficult, Lew stayed at her farm that night. She woke every hour until five AM, when she gave up. Her first urge was to check with Bruce or Lisa Carter to see if either had succeeded in confirming the DNA match, but she managed to persuade herself that it was too early.

To her surprise, her personal cell phone rang shortly before six and it was Bruce. "Chief, no news yet, and I knew you'd be waiting by the phone. Marathon County had a huge meth bust yesterday with three officers shot and the suspects still on the run. We've got everyone available working the Marathon crisis. I'm afraid yours is on the back burner until we've got some control over that situation. Want you to know you're up the minute we can manage that."

"I understand, Bruce." Lew hung up, frustrated. She had been hoping to have an arrest warrant ready by late that morning. Now it looked more like afternoon.

A knock on the kitchen door surprised her. "Aunt Lew?" called Bridget through the screen door. "Hope I'm not waking you." She walked into the kitchen where Lew was sitting at the wooden table with a cup of coffee in front of her.

"Do I look like I'm sleeping?" Lew kidded her, even though she saw worry on the young woman's face. "I'm a wreck, Bridget. Come on in and let me fix you some breakfast. But first tell me why you're here today. I was expecting you tomorrow. Wait, one thing before I forget—you've got to get that envelope with the lawsuit files to Rich Hartman today. He about had a nervous breakdown when he couldn't find it in your father's file cabinet."

"Oh, sorry. I didn't think about that. I should have taken it to him before going back for exams, darn it. Classes ended late yesterday, and I can't stand having my clothes and my precious stuff from childhood still at the house with that woman. I worry she'll throw it out or something. So I'm going over this morning to pack up the rest of my things. I'll put some in storage—"

"And leave some here with me," said Lew, giving her a hug and pushing her down into a chair at the table. "Want help? I've got a little time this morning."

"That would be terrific."

*Terrific for both of us*, thought Lew, *something to take my mind off waiting for the damn DNA results.*

Within thirty minutes they were driving into town in Lew's pickup. As they neared the house, Bridget put a hand on Lew's arm, "Uh-oh, I see that man's car in our driveway. I won't go in if he's there. Wait, I know. Aunt Lew, go around the back way and park behind the house."

"In the neighbor's yard?"

"In the empty lot that's next door to the house behind ours. We can park there and go through the backyard. I've got a key for the back door to the garage. I'm sure Linda keeps the hall door closed, so she won't even see us coming and going from my room."

Bridget flashed her aunt a guilty smile as she said, "That's how I snuck out of the house back when I was in high school. Mom and Dad never knew. Pretty handy now, huh? Never trust a teenager."

"I like going in the back way. So long as you have a key we're doing nothing wrong," said Lew. She wasn't anxious to meet up with Stan either, and she knew that the master bedroom and bath were at the opposite end of house. The door to the hall, which led to Pete's den, Bridget's bedroom, and the entry to the garage was kept closed to keep out drafts and mice from the garage.

Lew parked in the empty lot and followed Bridget as she crossed the yard carrying a couple of boxes for her things. They slipped inside the garage, took off their wet shoes, opened the door to the hallway, and padded silently down the hall to Bridget's bedroom.

Once inside, Bridget directed Lew to empty her bureau drawers while she tackled the clothes hanging in her closet before scooping books and prized keepsakes from the shelves around her bed. They worked quietly and had nearly filled the two large boxes when they heard loud voices.

"Someone's in the hall," said Bridget in a whisper.

"Sssh." Lew put a finger to her lips.

Steps grew closer, and they could hear Linda shouting, "I don't believe you. There is no reason why you can't take me, too."

"They're by the coat closet. He must be leaving," whispered Bridget.

The closet was right next to her bedroom, and they could hear the voices clearly along with the sound of the closet door opening and closing.

"I'll give you a call later this evening, sweetheart," said Stan.

Ignoring his remark, Linda said, "I told you I want to go along tonight. Please? Be fun to meet your old friends."

"Oh, for heaven's sake, this is *my* class reunion," said Stan in a wheedling tone. "You'd be bored out of your mind."

"No I wouldn't. Be fun to find out more about you," said Linda.

Silence. Then Stan: "Look, I'm going by myself."

"No, you're not." Linda's voice was louder, angry. "I heard you on that call last night—you're going with that old girlfriend of yours!"

The voices had started to fade. The hall door must have closed.

Sound of the front door slamming and a car starting.

Lew heard footsteps pounding down the hallway toward the kitchen. She could imagine what Linda might be thinking: now that Stan was about to be worth a lot of money, she needed to protect her property.

"Let's get out of here," whispered Bridget. "I've got the important stuff."

"Wait," said Lew. "She is so upset." Without waiting for Bridget to say anything, Lew opened the bedroom door and called out, "Linda? Bridget and I are back here moving her things . . ." She waited.

More footsteps and the door to the hallway opened. "What the hell are you doing sneaking in here?"

"Do you need help?" asked Lew, ignoring the woman's angry accusation.

Linda advanced down the hallway until she was standing in front of them. She threw a look at Bridget's boxes, then gave an angry shrug.

"No, I do not need help. What I do need is for you to leave thank you." She turned to walk away, then paused to look back at them. Lew saw a glimmer of malice in the woman's eyes. *Stan had better be careful.*

* * *

Lew didn't get to her office until after eight, which was late for her. She had helped Bridget move her boxes into the old barn and made sure the fridge had enough food for her new roommate.

"Go to work, Aunt Lew," Bridget had said as she was finishing a piece of toast. "I'll be fine. I have a meeting with Mr. Hartman to give him the files, and later I'm having dinner with my friend Brenda. Don't worry about me, okay?"

"Fine," said Lew. "But keep your cell phone close by in case I need to reach you." She didn't want to share her hopes for the DNA results until she could be sure.

"Will do," said Bridget, waving the iPhone she had set on the kitchen table. "Now scram."

Lew chuckled, gave her a quick hug, and headed out. The rain, which had let up while they were carrying the boxes to the barn, had decided to drench the Northwoods again. Splashing through large puddles along the dirt lane leading from her farmhouse to the highway, Lew worried that Loon Lake might have serious flooding if the rain didn't let up soon.

On the way into town, she checked with Marlaine on Dispatch to see if there were flood warnings for the area.

"Not yet, Chief," said Marlaine, "but I had so much water on my road as I drove in that I felt like I was going to lose traction. I'm telling everyone to please slow down."

\* \* \*

After going through the morning updates, Lew called the officer watching the Hartmans' home and driveway.

"Morning, Chief," said Todd Donovan. "No news, quiet out here. Rich walked out to get his morning paper and we chatted for a few minutes. Otherwise, it's real quiet. I relieved Officer Adamczak at seven, and he said it had been a quiet night too."

Lew shuffled more papers, shifted a thousand times in her chair, and when she couldn't stand it any longer called Bruce Peters.

"Sorry, Chief, no news yet but should be soon. Our investigators are close to wrapping up work at the crime scene over in Marathon County. Your case is next. I know it's an emergency so I'm checking with my techs every half-hour or so."

The minute she ended that conversation, a call from Charlotte showed up on her personal cell phone. "Lew? Have you got Stan?"

"Not yet, still waiting on the DNA results. A matter of hours, Charlotte. Please be patient."

"I'm trying. Johnny's got school all day today so maybe by three o'clock, you think?"

Lew exhaled. "I'm hoping. Keep you posted. You know not to say anything, right?"

"Of course." The stress in her voice was so obvious that Lew knew she needn't worry.

The call from Bruce came in at a quarter past three. He confirmed the DNA match between Stanley Mayer and the DNA found on the pry bar and the golf club. He also confirmed that skin cells from the sweatshirt found in Grace McDonough's trash provided DNA matches to both Grace McDonough and Stan Mayer.

"While it was not a confirmation that it had been used to smother her, it's a strong indication that it may have been. One more finding of interest to you, Chief—bloodstains on the floor of the garage belong to Noah McDonough. My forensic tech is confident that that is where he was when stabbed with the broken golf club. The golf bag that had held the club was leaning against a wall only ten feet from the bloodstains."

Osborne was sitting across the desk from Lew when she heard from Bruce. He could tell from the expression on her face that it was time for her to request a warrant for the arrest of Stan Mayer. He listened as she called the judge's office.

She had the warrant in hand within minutes, and they left the Loon Lake police department together. Knowing that both her officers were busy with their surveillance of the Hartman family, Osborne offered to go with her. She turned him down.

He balked. "No, Lewellyn, if you're going to arrest Stanley Mayer, it would be wise to have backup, especially in this weather. This rain can make the sidewalks slippery, and even if you're armed that's no guarantee that Stan Mayer won't do something dangerous."

"All right," said Lew. Doc had a point. She was well aware that she could handle the arrest on her own, but she had a department policy that, in the event of a serious crime, arresting officers should always have backup.

Osborne was right: she needed backup.

"You'll need your gun, Doc," she said as they approached their cars in the parking lot.

"Got it in a lockbox in my glove compartment," said Osborne. "I'll grab it."

After Lew had parked her cruiser in front of the building where Stan's office was, Osborne followed her up the narrow stairway. Though he knew better, he worried about her going ahead of him—this woman who had brought him back to life. *Dear God*, he prayed, *keep her safe. Please.*

"Do you expect Stan to be armed?" he whispered when they reached the landing. Lew shrugged.

"I'm ready if he is," she said. "But this is going to take him by surprise. He doesn't know we found the pry bar and the golf club. Ready?"

She knocked on the door marked "Mayer Appraisals."
No answer.

She knocked again.

Silence. Ten seconds passed. Lew tried the brass handle on the office door. It wasn't locked. She pressed down and pushed the door open slightly. "Hello, Stan?" No answer.

She pushed the door open wider and tried again, "Hello, Stan? Are you in?"

Then Lew pushed the door wide open, and Osborne followed her into the office. It was empty. The late afternoon sun was the only light in the room.

Osborne looked around. Stan's office was a mess. Unopened mail and papers were strewn across the old oak desk. The shade on a small lamp on the shelf behind the desk was askew and looked to be permanently that way. A worn athletic jacket bearing the Loon Lake High letters was thrown over a chair in one corner. A wastebasket next to the chair was overflowing with loose papers, fast-food wrappers, and beer cans.

"Let's check his house," said Lew. She ran down the stairs so fast that Osborne tripped twice and nearly fell down trying to keep up with her.

# Chapter Twenty-Eight

～

Margie studied herself in the full-length mirror. It was the third outfit she had tried on. *Yes*, she thought. *These narrow-legged black pants make me look a lot slimmer. And the black top too. Yes, this outfit hides what needs to be hidden. And I'm sure I'll look a hell of a lot better than most of the women at the reunion. I. Am. Not. Fat.* She treated herself to a satisfied smile, then checked her watch. *Whoa, four thirty—I better hurry.* She ducked into the bathroom for a final tooth brushing, picked up the hand mirror to check her hair from behind, and grabbed an umbrella from the coat closet. She waited. Checked her watch again, And waited some more.

*Jeez*, thinking back to her phone conversation. *Didn't Stan say he would pick me up at four forty-five? Did I get that wrong?"*

She decided to wait by the front window. Peering through the rain, which had picked up in the last half-hour, she made a mental note to leave her front door unlocked. Rain was forecast to last until early in the morning, and she didn't need to be standing in a downpour struggling to put a key in the lock when Stan dropped her off later.

*And if I get lucky that'll make it easy for the two of us to run inside . . . if I invite him in. And then who knows . . . ?* Margie smiled to herself. She was ready for a change; she deserved to get lucky.

Four fifty . . . four fifty-five. Had he forgotten?

Before she could let her heart break, a text came in on her phone.

It was Stan: "Running late, be there in . . ."

That was all. She sighed with relief. And waited.

# Chapter
# Twenty-Nine

Siren off, Lew sped past the old landfill to the asphalt road leading up to the house that Stan had rented after Charlotte kicked him out. The old place was in dire need of a paint job; the front porch railing was hanging loose and it was obvious Stan had no interest in lawn care.

A rundown garage, fifty feet from the house, leaned sideways. What had once been a garage door appeared to be stuck open, exposing two plastic garbage cans and a small fishing boat on a rusty trailer. Stan's Honda SUV was nowhere in sight.

After Lew parked and jumped out of the cruiser, Osborne jogged after her. The rain mixed with hail made the cracked flagstones leading to the front porch slippery. Lew waited for him at the front door. She knocked and the door slid open. She threw a quizzical look at Osborne.

"Hello-o-o," she called. Osborne could sense that she wasn't expecting an answer. "I don't have a search warrant, Doc. We can't go in."

"He's not here anyway."

Lew turned to hurry back to the cruiser. "I am so glad Charlotte got the kid out of the way," she said as she ran. "Awful to have your father arrested in front of you. Be bad enough when Charlotte has to tell him the truth."

Once in the car, Lew called Dispatch. "Marlaine? Put out an APB for Stan Mayer, will you please? He's wanted on suspicion of murder. With a warning that he may be armed."

They were driving back to the police station, hail battering the roof of the cruiser, when Marlaine's voice came on the police radio to say that Stan Mayer's car had been located. "I'll patch you through to the officer at the scene," she said. "One of the sheriff's deputies found him. Deputy's name is Gordy."

Within seconds Lew was on the line with the deputy. "Got Mayer?"

"Yes, Chief, sure do—"

She didn't wait for him to say more before asking, "Where is he?"

"Under his car. We're out on County C, and a passing motorist called 911. The roadway is flooded right here and . . . he must have taken the corner too fast and hydroplaned over the ditch and into the trees. I'm looking at the vehicle right now. Gotta tell ya, Chief, between that hailstorm and these bald tires—no wonder the guy lost traction."

"If that sonofabitch thinks he's hiding from you," Lew shouted into the mouthpiece of her radio, "do whatever to stop him. Do not let him run!"

"No need to worry, Chief Ferris. He's not going anywhere—he's dead."

Lew was quiet for a long minute. She and Osborne stared at one another, stunned.

"Chief Ferris? Did I lose you?" asked the deputy, his voice crackling over the police radio.

"No, I'm here. I'll be there in a few minutes."

"Got it, Chief. We called for an ambulance and they're just pulling up. I'll let them know. Got a call in to Ed Pecore, too. Figured you'd need the coroner here."

"Forget that drunk," said Lew, not surprised to hear a low chuckle from the deputy. Few people in Loon Lake did not know about Pecore's over-served issues. "I've got Doc Osborne with me, and he's our acting coroner so we're covered."

"One more thing, Chief. I've got the victim's cell phone. It was thrown out of the vehicle when it crashed and looks like he was in the middle of texting someone named Margie. Is that his wife? Should someone call that individual?"

"It's not his wife. Hold onto it until I get there."

\* \* \*

It was after six when Lew returned to her office. She laid Stan Mayer's cell phone, encased in an evidence bag, on her desk and collapsed into her desk chair.

"Chief?" Dani poked her head in the door. "What a day, huh?"

"Come in," said Lew. "Why are you here so late?"

"After you told me to ask the Wausau boys to search Stan Mayer's office and house, I thought I'd hang around in case they came up with his laptop or desk computer. Figured you'd want me to check it out."

"Tomorrow will be fine. You heard he died a few hours ago in a car accident, right?"

"I did. When I heard what had happened I called the tire shop and made an appointment to have mine checked and rotated. What's that?" She pointed to the cell phone on Lew's desk.

"Flew out of Stan Mayer's car during the accident. But it's an iPhone, so I doubt we'll have any luck seeing what's on it, dammit."

"Umm," said Dani. "Be nice if we had his password, wouldn't it?"

Lew stared at her. "Yes it would." She picked up her cell phone and punched in Charlotte's number. While she waited for Charlotte to answer, she covered the mouthpiece and said, "You know kids. A month ago Doc's grandson used his dad's phone to order three video games. Got punished but that was a wake-up call for his folks. I wonder about John Mayer—hi, Charlotte, Lew here."

She had called Charlotte from the scene of the accident, knowing it would be a shock for young John and his mother. Charlotte may have been furious with Stan's behavior over the years but she would never have wished him dead. At least that's what Lew assumed. She knew that she'd never know for sure, and she would certainly never ask.

"Quick question—would you or your son happen to know Stan's password for opening his phone?"

"I don't, never have," said Charlotte, "but let me ask Johnny." Lew could hear voices in the background, then Charlotte came back on the phone. "Got pencil and paper to write this down? It's 325523."

Lew repeated the number back to her, and Dani scribbled it down too.

"A variation of Johnny's birthday," said Charlotte, her voice so quiet Lew could barely hear her.

"Thank you. I'll let you know if we find anything."

Dani reached for the evidence bag containing the phone. "I've got nitrile gloves in my desk so I'll be careful, Chief. You want to know what I find tonight? You look exhausted."

"Are you kidding? Don't feel you have to work until midnight, but if you do find something this evening please let me know."

Before leaving her office, Lew made two phone calls, letting Officers Donovan and Adamczak know they were free to get a good night's sleep.

# Chapter Thirty

After a late dinner with Doc, Lew drove home. She didn't want to leave Bridget all alone so soon after losing her father. That may have been thoughtful on Lew's part, but Bridget didn't even get to her place until after eleven that night. When she started to apologize, Lew waved a hand to stop her, saying, "Don't be silly, kiddo, old friends are just what you need at a time like this. But now that you're here, I'm going to sleep. So see you in the morning." And giving her niece a warm hug, Lew went off to bed.

Before falling asleep, she made one last check of her cell phone: no message from Dani.

* * *

When Lew woke up she was surprised at how soundly she had slept; it was her best night's sleep since Pete's death. Even though it was early—shortly after five AM— she was wide awake and anxious to get going.

Taking care not to disturb Bridget, she dressed and drove into town. The rain had stopped, though roads were still wet. The sky overhead was soft, with washes of pale violet edged with a lemon yellow—a pastel kind of morning—and Lew noticed it all. This was a good sign, as up to now she had paid little attention to spring's valiant efforts to force May into June. As she drove, the sky brightened, and for the first time in weeks she had a thought that lifted her heart: trout fishing would be excellent this weekend.

With that thought she made a mental note to alert Bruce to that possibility, but, more important, to plan to join her for a press conference later that day. She might not have all the answers she wanted, but people at least needed to know that the questions of who had killed Grace and Noah McDonough and Peter Ferris had been answered.

Walking into her office at a quarter to six, she was surprised to find she was not alone. Two people sat waiting: Doc had doughnuts and coffee, and Dani had a look on her face—Lew called it "that look"—which meant that something significant had happened.

"Dani first, then doughnut," said Osborne before Lew could open her mouth.

Dani didn't wait for Lew to sit down but got to her feet, holding a cell phone face out so Lew could see it.

"I found this number, Chief. Stan got a call from this number at 4:10 AM Wednesday May 20, the morning your brother was killed. Does it look familiar?"

Lew studied the number. "No . . . it's looks a little familiar maybe, but it isn't one I know right off the bat."

She pulled over one of the chairs from around the table at the end of the room and sat down beside Dani. "It does look familiar . . . the more I think . . . I'm sure I've seen it before."

She had her personal cell phone out and began to scroll through calls she had received recently. Dani sat silent beside her.

"Nothing yesterday . . . or the day before . . . here, Tuesday—I see it." Lew's voice rose with excitement. "I got a call Tuesday morning from that number, and wait— yes, that's when Linda called at the last minute to tell me she was having the memorial service for Pete that afternoon."

"I've already traced that number," said Dani, "and you're right. That number belongs to Linda Jarvis."

"That's Linda's name from her first marriage. She didn't change it after she married Pete."

"I thought that might be the case," said Dani.

"Doughnut?" asked Osborne as he handed one to her, aware that Lewellyn Ferris was not likely to sit still in one place for long. She grabbed it and hurried to her desk.

Mouth full of doughnut, Lew checked the time. "Damn! I hate to wake up Judge Martin this early."

"Give him until seven," said Osborne. "Nothing will change before now and then."

\* \* \*

Shortly before nine AM Lew pulled into the driveway in front of her brother's home. Relieved to have been asked to accompany her for backup, Osborne sat in the passenger's seat.

"I'm worried, Lewellyn," he said. "Intent as you are on arresting Linda, and even though the law would appear to be on your side, are you sure that because the victim was your brother you might not have a conflict of interest? One that could jeopardize the case against this woman?"

"You're right, Doc, that is an important issue. I've already thought about it, but I'm going ahead here. I have to know how Pete was set up and why. I have to know. I don't care if Linda Jarvis goes to prison. I just need to know.

Lew knocked on the door that had once opened to warmth and welcome but now . . . sadness and anger. Osborne, alert to what could happen next, stood ready to protect her.

Still in pajamas, Linda cracked open the door. The face that reminded Lew of a wizened monkey looked so much more so without makeup. Nor was there any sign of tears having been shed—no redness around the eyes. She was holding a cell phone in her hand and gestured to indicate that Lew was interrupting her in the middle of a conversation.

When Lew stepped forward to push the door open, Linda lowered the hand that held the phone and spat out, "Dammit, Lewellyn, what the hell are you doing coming here so early?"

"You're under arrest as an accomplice to the murder of Peter Ferris," answered Lew, her voice calm. "I have a warrant for your arrest and a search of your home. Please hand over that phone." With the phone safe in her left hand, Lew then read the woman her rights.

One hour later, Dani confirmed that a call had been made from Linda Jarvis's cell phone to Stanley Mayer's cell phone at 4:10 AM on Wednesday, May 20.

*   *   *

Linda was seated across from Lew in the interrogation room at the Loon Lake police department.

"I did not kill your brother. I was nowhere near where he was found, and I can prove it."

Lew ignored her. "You called Stan to let him know that Pete had left the house. Knowing that, Stan drove out to the lake, where he knew Pete would be checking on the loon nest. We have visual evidence of Stan on the trail cameras following Pete down toward the nest. We have Stan's DNA on the pry bar used to kill Pete. We also have Stan's DNA on the broken golf club used to kill Noah McDonough, and I am sure we will find evidence that Stan smothered Grace McDonough before putting her body in her Range Rover and driving it off the bridge. We have the evidence, Linda. If you can tell us why Stan did this, the court may go easier on you. Right now, however, you are an accessory to the murder of Peter Ferris, and you may be looking at life in prison."

Muscles in the monkey face quivered. Linda stared down at the top of the table in front of her—downward so Lew couldn't see her eyes.

That was okay with Lew. She knew what was going through Linda's mind and decided to needle her, saying, "If you don't want to talk, I'll find out what I need to know when I meet with Margery Caldwell. My impression is that Stan told her everything." She knew this wasn't likely, but then who knew? Maybe he had. The tactic was worth a try.

"That's who that was? Margie Caldwell? My God," said Linda. "She's married. She's fat. Why—"

"Recently divorced," said Lew. "Walked away with quite a nice financial settlement too. She may be fat, but she's also wealthy." That was not a lie.

The monkey face twisted with anger. Linda closed her eyes and shook her head. Lew sat silent, waiting.

"What happens to me if I'm able to help with the investigation?"

"Did you call Stan that morning?"

A long pause. Life in prison? Linda was not stupid. "Yes, I called him, but not why you think."

"What am I thinking?"

Linda ignored the question. "I called Stan because he had been hoping to get time alone with Pete to negotiate. Pete was always gone fishing or with that goddamn Loon Rescue or hanging out with Rich, and Stan just needed to have some time alone with him."

"Negotiate what? Pete wasn't selling anything."

"Stan thought that if Pete knew how much money the McDonough property would be worth to Normandy Mining—and if Stan promised to cut him and Rich in for a percentage after the sale—they would drop the lawsuit."

"But Stan didn't own the land. How could he be in a position to negotiate? Grace wouldn't have agreed to that—would she?"

Linda shut her eyes, fear rippling across her face. Her mouth was closed tight and twitching. She had made a mistake.

Lew softened her voice and leaned back in her chair. "How did you know Grace wouldn't be a party to the negotiation? Linda . . . how did you know that Stan would be the person to profit from that sale?"

Linda said nothing. She continued to sit with her eyes closed and her body trembling.

"The more you tell me the easier it'll go," said Lew.

"You promise?" It was a whisper.

"I'll do what I can, and you've known me long enough to know that I'm fair."

"Yes, I know that."

The woman straightened up. She took a deep breath and exhaled.

"It started last summer when Stan ran into Grace at a bar and bought her a beer. Then she bought him a beer, and the two of them had a good six or more until they both got good and drunk. That's when she took him up on his offer to appraise her property. She said she was being offered a lot of money by a sulfide mining group and needed good advice. So Stan looked into the deal and offered to broker it for her."

Linda looked at Lew as she said, "He took a piece of crap-ass land on the river worth no mor'n thirty thousand bucks, talked it up with Normandy Mining, and let 'em sneak in for a test. He worked it to where he had Normandy offering Grace minimum thirty million—minimum."

Linda sputtered. "He told me it could even be fifty million once they did their testing legitimately. Fifty million bucks and you wonder why Stan wanted a piece? When he found out it could be worth that much, he obsessed. Just obsessed. His mom had told him before she died who his father was. Knowing that drove Stan nuts. He couldn't believe the old man never put him in the will."

"Had he ever met Edward McDonough?"

"No, and that made him even madder. He said the old man treated his mother like she was a prostitute." Linda looked up now. "She wasn't. She was his mistress for over four years."

"I can understand Stan's fury," said Lew.

"Fury? Fury? What Stan felt was a hell of a lot more than fury. I told him he was right too."

"Not much you can do about that, though," said Lew.

"Now that is not true," said Linda, pounding the table with one fist. "Stan researched wills and estates and found out that if he hadn't been specifically excluded from the old man's will he would have been a legitimate heir."

"Along with Grace and Noah?"

"Yes. All he needed was DNA proof."

"Oh, so he asked her to take a test?"

"Yes, I told him about Ancestry DNA and 23andMe and how we could prove their connection. So one night when they were drinking together, he asked Grace to spit into one of those Ancestry tubes. He tried to make it a joke and cajole her into it, but she refused. She wouldn't hear of it.

"All summer, all last fall, as Stan gave her excellent appraisal and negotiating advice, I know he asked her at least once more, but she still refused. I told him to steal her toothbrush and do it on the sly, but that woman was canny. She barely let him in the house, much less her bathroom.

"The closer he got to finalizing the deal for Grace, the more frustrated Stan got. When he told me what he was thinking of doing, I told him he needed to be absolutely sure that they were biologically related. That's when he remembered getting the gene test at the Holder Clinic and how that genetic counselor had told him she did family detective stuff on the side. Stan said she had been really, really nice to him—like she had a crush on him or something—so he made an appointment and charmed her into telling him how to get a DNA sample from a dead person. After that he had a plan.

"So Stan got Grace really, really plowed the night she got that offer from Normandy Mining—so slammed she fell asleep, as he knew she would. He was getting her into her car when she woke up, and he had to do something . . ."

"You mean wrap that sweatshirt around her head?"

"He wanted it to be painless. She would never know, y'know?" Linda looked at Lew for reassurance that that had been a good thing. "That's when Noah drove into the garage, and Stan had to do more."

"Of course."

Listening, Lew realized that Stan hadn't gone down to the loon nest to negotiate with Pete. He'd gone there determined to kill him. With Pete out of the way, it would take months if not years to challenge the Normandy deal. After what happened to Pete, Rich Hartman was sure to think twice about pursuing the case against Normandy Mining. Was it worth his life—the lives of his wife and children?

*Stan had a plan all right*, thought Lew as she listened to Linda. *First Pete, then Grace and Noah. He had a plan, and he knew it was perfect. Like so many criminals, he was convinced of his own brilliance.*

"After Grace's accident and the DNA test results from the Holder Clinic, the bank believed everything. So Stan was set."

"Except for Noah," said Lew. "What was his plan for Noah?"

"That was the easy part, Stan said. Noah might overdose on drugs or drown or maybe commit suicide. Even if Noah was around, Stan could still sell the property. He wasn't in any rush to get rid of Noah until the time felt right.

"But when Noah walked into the garage and saw his mom dead, Stan had to think fast. He remembered that old shack 'cause he'd found it when he was walking the property for the appraisal. It was hidden so far back that he was sure no one would ever find the old place. At least not before the critters got to it."

Linda shook her head. "So when Stan heard those kids had found the body that was a big surprise. Still, he knew there'd be no way anyone could know who had killed Noah. Stan said he told the guys at the bank it had to be one of Noah's drug buddies, maybe one of the dealers that drive up from Milwaukee.

"See, Stan was meeting with the bankers every day after Grace died. He said they trusted him, especially after they heard that Noah was a sexual predator. At first, when Noah was missing and before his body was found, the bank had told Stan that, as he was legally heir to the estate, he didn't need Noah's approval to sell some of the property. He told the bank that if and when Noah decided to show up, they would both be heirs and could share any proceeds from the sale equally. That made sense to everyone."

"Linda," said Lew, "did it ever occur to you that Stan was making a mistake in thinking he could get away with . . . with murder?"

Linda's face fell. "I guess it did at first. But Stan's a smart man. The more he told me, the more I figured he could make it work. He had a backup plan too. Just never got to use it."

"Hiding in Canada with all the money?"

"Um . . . actually we were going to Mexico. A little town down there where Stan vacationed once. Warm, by the ocean. We could drive and be there in three to four days."

Lew nodded. "You're right. That could've worked." She knew she was lying again, but a little encouragement might not hurt.

"Do you think I was duped?" asked Linda, surprising Lew with the question.

"I think—" Lew wanted to be sure she said the right thing and, hiding her urge to wince, said, "You were in a hard place. What could you do?" She knew she wasn't making much sense, but she wanted to keep Linda talking. For her brother's sake, she *had* to keep the woman talking. "So what went wrong?"

"You mean why did Stan die? He did it to himself. We had a fight yesterday afternoon, and I told him if he was thinking of dumping me to forget it or I'd . . ." She didn't finish.

Again, the stare down at the tabletop, the twitching along the monkey-like cheekbones. Then Linda looked into Lew's eyes. "I heard it in his voice that night when he invited that what's-her-name, Margie, to dinner."

"When was that supposed to happen?"

"Last night, some stupid reunion thing with old friends. He said it wasn't anything, but I knew. When he said I couldn't go along—hell, I knew for sure then. A woman knows, y'know?"

Lew nodded in total agreement. *Yes, a woman knows.*

"He even tried to borrow my car, but I was damned if I'd let him do that. He could impress his girlfriend with his own crap car."

"Did you tell him that?"

"No. I was so angry I just . . ." She shook her head. "I just told him to get the hell out of there." A pause, then Linda said, "He tried to tell me I was overreacting and he'd come back to my place after the dinner. I didn't believe him."

"Well," said Lew softly, "he didn't come back, did he?"

* * *

She escorted Linda out of the interrogation room and into the hands of the policewoman waiting to take her down to a cell. Lew was exhausted. Sad, drained, but relieved that now she finally knew the facts.

# Chapter
# Thirty-One

❧

Lew sat at her desk waiting for Bruce to arrive for the press conference at three. She checked her watch. With half an hour to go, she called Rich Hartman. "You heard the news, of course," she said when he answered. "Linda Jarvis is going to be looking for a lawyer, but I don't think you'll be on her short list."

"No, you're right about that," he said, chuckling. "But with everything that's happened I'm wondering what will happen to all that land owned by the McDonough family. What I do know is that the sale to Normandy Mining has been put on hold, so that's a relief—for the moment."

"That's why I'm calling. I was hoping Bridget had stopped by with the files you were looking for—the ones Pete kept in the brown envelope.

"She did, and thank you, Chief. I told her I owe her whatever legal help she may need in the next fifty years." Rich sounded like he'd won the lottery. "Do you know what this means? Having these files will save me hours of work. Thanks to Pete's documentation on the impact that sulfide mining can have on water systems, we now have a shot at saving the Pelican River."

*   *   *

The reporters were waiting at three o'clock as scheduled. This time news had reached Wausau, and there were three TV reporters, one from Rhinelander and two from Wausau, along with reporters from the Wausau newspaper and the *Rhinelander Daily News*.

Lew and Bruce were ready with statements and willing to answer questions. A few bystanders were there too, including Dani, Osborne, and Erin. Osborne and Erin had walked over together from her house, which was just down the block from the courthouse.

Lew opened the session, saying, "I want everyone to know that Loon Lake owes a huge thank-you to Bruce Peters and his Wausau boys. Without their extraordinary DNA expertise and technology—" Lew stopped herself, then said, "Sorry, I take that back. Dr. Lisa Carter played a critical role in helping my department find the individual responsible for the deaths of three people. As Dr. Carter is the new forensic pathologist for the Wausau Crime Lab," Lew paused, and with a wide smile said, "I sure can't call them 'the Wausau boys anymore,' can I?" She gestured toward Bruce, "So, Mr. Peters, will you please let Dr. Carter know how much we appreciate her hard work?"

After Lew had answered questions relating to the arrest of Linda Jarvis, the death of Stanley Mayer, and his role in the murders of three people, the reporter from the Rhinelander television station had one last question.

"Chief Ferris, what is the status of your campaign for sheriff of McBride County? Do you think you have a good shot at winning the election?"

Lew was caught off guard. "I—I—that has been last on my to-do list these past few days." She saw Erin standing off to one side of the group. She couldn't miss her grimace.

After the reporters left, Erin approached her, arms folded and a serious expression on her face. "We've got exactly ten days—"

"I'm dropping out of the race," said Lew.

"What?" Erin recoiled as if slapped across the face. "That doesn't make sense."

Lew caught Doc's eye. His expression was noncommittal. "I'm sure Chief Ferris has a good reason," he said, clearing his throat. "Right?"

"My reason is very simple," said Lew, waving a hand in the direction of Dani and Bruce, who were standing there looking as stunned as Erin.

"I don't want to lose working with people who are very good at what they do and who are," she pursed her lips before saying, ". . . who are good friends as well as talented colleagues."

"But why does being sheriff change that?" asked Erin.

"Because that position is nothing but administrative BS, that's why. I like working closely on cases, seeing the people—good and bad—who are involved, the people whom I might be able to help. I do not want to spend the next ten years doing budgets, debating policy, and arguing with . . . community leaders." Lew spat out the last two words, making it clear that she equated "community leaders" with "politicians."

"And I wouldn't be able to work hands-on with people like Dani and Bruce," she added.

"Not true," interjected Bruce. "The Wausau Crime Lab works with the Sheriff's Department." He grinned. "I just happen to prioritize you, Chief Ferris—and you know why. By the way, thanks for the invite for Saturday. I'll drive up, and Lisa Carter wants to come too."

"Chief Ferris?" asked Dani. "What if I applied to be your senior admin and run IT for the county as well as Loon Lake? Would that help?"

Now it was Lew's turn to be taken aback. "Oh . . . I hadn't thought of that."

Erin's grimace morphed into an expression of happy anticipation.

# Chapter Thirty-Two

❧

Lew caught her breath: perched on a leaf of tag alder not two feet from where she had paused to study the hatch of Blue Wing Olives was a dragonfly, sunlight shimmering on its wings. Her heart soared.

She had arrived early at the clearing along the Prairie River. At first she was disappointed with the bright sunshine. She preferred it chilly, dark, and overcast, with a threat of rain even though it had been raining for three days now. So she was surprised to see such a glorious hatch.

A Toyota van pulled up to park alongside her pickup. Bruce and Lisa jumped out, waved to Lew, and reached into the back of the van for their gear.

"It's a size sixteen day—maybe a size twenty-two," said Lew, referring to the size of the hooks on the trout flies. "Dry flies today," she added as she pulled her fly-fishing vest on. She pointed an index finger at Bruce.

"Hey, you, be sure you've got that Adams ready. I'm tired of reminding you it's the buggiest-looking dry fly you got."

"Chief keeps hammering on me what size trout fly to use," Bruce said to Lisa, who had a confused look on her face.

"And he never listens," said Lew shaking her head in defeat.

Bruce looked out across the narrow stream and nodded in Lew's direction, "Whoa, what a hatch. Are we lucky or what?"

"I see Blue Wing Olive mayflies along with Pale Morning Duns and some caddis flies," said Lew. "Doesn't get much better than this. Seize the moment."

"Don't worry," said Bruce, assuring Lisa, "you only need another ten years of study to know what we're talking about."

"Shut up, Bruce," said Lew, "you'll drive her to bait fishing. Lisa, remember this: you don't always have to know what you're doing to catch a few trout. And speaking as an instructor, let me say a day like today is made for fishing with dry flies. In my world, I believe fly rods were made for this: a dry fly on a tapered leader and a floating line. Sheer elegance."

"Elegance? Funny word for fishing," said Lisa as she pulled on her waders.

"You'll know what I mean within an hour," said Lew. "Need a review of what I showed you the last time we were out here?"

"Nope, I think I'm good to go," said Lisa. "I've been putting myself to sleep reading Joan Wulff's *Fly Casting Techniques*." She gave Lew a big grin, the kind of grin a third-grader gives when they can recite the names of all fifty states.

At that moment Osborne pulled up in his Subaru. He got out and walked down to the riverbank where Lew was waiting for Bruce and Lisa. Lew was watching him head her way when he stopped suddenly and pointed. She turned to look in that direction and gasped. "Bruce! Lisa! Stop what you're doing—look!"

Trout weren't rising—they were leaping. The mayfly hatch was so tantalizing that even the fish were beside themselves.

"Put your rods down and watch," said Lew. "You rarely see this. Doc, have I told you lately that I love you?"

Osborne grinned, He knew she knew she'd have missed the magic if he hadn't stopped and pointed.

Lewellyn Ferris had experienced a grave loss with the death of her beloved brother, and Doc knew the sight of brook trout leaping in the Prairie River was one of the few things that might ease her grief.

Astounding as the sight of the trout leaping was, it was too brief. Within seconds the fish changed tactics.

Seeming to ignore the hatch that had dazzled them, now they lurked beneath the riffles, teasing.

* * *

The four of them had just begun to wade upstream, with Lew instructing Lisa: "Don't watch Bruce, he does it wrong. Okay, now lift that forearm and fly reel as if they're glued together . . ." She was in the midst of instructing when Ray's battered blue pickup skidded into the clearing.

Climbing out of the truck, he reached back for his hat, which he crammed down on his head as he skipped along the riverbank waving his arms.

Lew heard Lisa laughing at the sight. She shook her head. If she hadn't seen the six foot four fishing guide with the stuffed trout on his head a thousand times, she would have laughed too. But, comic hat aside, Ray rarely did anything to dampen the day. This was no exception. "Hel-lo-o-o there," he called, and gestured for his friends to come closer.

"Hey, Ray, thank you for the bluegills you left at my back door last night," said Osborne, reminding Lew of the delicious meal they had enjoyed.

"You're as welcome as the flowers. Say, Lisa, did you hear about the guy who went to the lumberyard and said, 'I want a two-by-four.' 'How long do you want it?' asked the owner. 'I wanna keep it, whaddya think?'"

After a pause, Lisa laughed. Everyone else had already heard the joke.

"And did you hear about the chameleon who couldn't change color? He had reptile dysfunction—"

"Enough," said Lisa, chuckling and a little embarrassed by the attention. "Please, someone, shut that man up!"

"Ray, do you have something to tell us?" asked Lew. "No more jokes, we got fish waiting."

"Okay, okay, but I got some great news today. Lisa, you were so good on my podcast the other night that I got 936,702 listeners. A record for podcasts about fishing."

"I'm sure," said Bruce drily. "Tell me, man, how many fishing podcasts are there?"

"Um, maybe six?" Ray was undaunted by the put-down. "But only one with a lovely female." Before anyone could make a critical remark, he went on, "So I got this call from an agent who wants to pitch the idea as a documentary for Netflix. Now that is cool." He studied their faces.

"Are you kidding? Are you saying you would want me in it?" asked Lisa.

"Only if you insist," said Ray, looking like he'd scored a good date for the evening. "How 'bout we talk later?"

He winked and headed back to his truck, where the leaping musky mounted on the hood seemed, in the bright sunlight, to wink like its owner.

As he pushed forward over the river rocks under his waders, Osborne shook his head in wonder. His neighbor never failed to surprise him. "Netflix sounds like a stretch to me," he said to Lew as he waded behind her.

"So did the podcast, and look how well that's working," she answered. "So long as he doesn't tell jokes, he may do okay."

Bruce and Lisa had overheard her and laughed so loud they scared off the trout.

# Chapter Thirty-Three

Lew, Bridget, and Osborne sat in the front row of folding chairs that had been set before the open grave. It wasn't how Lew had planned to spend her Friday morning, but when Rich Hartman called with his idea, she had wiped away a tear and agreed. Together she and Rich had put together the guest list.

As she waited, Lew remembered how her brother had chosen to have his late wife's ashes buried alongside the graves of their parents and her son. That was three years ago. Lew knew that he would choose to be buried there too.

"I still wonder what Linda was thinking when she rushed us all through that ridiculous event she called a 'memorial service,'" Rich had said when he stopped by Lew's office to plan the morning. "Your brother has had an impact on so many lives over the years. Acknowledging who he was and how he lived this way will help all of us better deal with how we lost him."

The list they drew up during that conversation included former colleagues from the college as well as students with whom Pete had kept in touch. And then there were the men and women he had worked with from Loon Rescue and the Pelican River Action Committee. At that point, Rich had said that, if she didn't mind, he would handle the rest of the planning, and Lew had agreed.

Now they were all arriving at St. Mary's Cemetery that sunny May morning. Watching people take their seats, Lew felt that Pete would have been surprised and honored. She knew she was.

Father Gleason, a close friend of Pete's since they had been in the same kindergarten class, spoke first and blessed the urn holding Pete's ashes. Then Rich talked about what Pete had discovered while researching the impact that sulfide mining might have on the lives of the people in Loon Lake.

"More will be said on that shortly," said Rich. "But first I am happy to announce that Loon Rescue and the Pelican River Action Committee have partnered to offer a scholarship in honor of Pete's work, which will be given every year to a college senior graduating in environmental studies and planning to continue graduate work in the field."

He sat down behind Lew and gave both her and Bridget reassuring pats on their shoulders. Bridget looked at her aunt quizzically, but Lew shrugged. She didn't know what was supposed to happen next. Everyone was quiet, waiting. Osborne, sitting on Lew's right, glanced at her with a faint smile.

Then two people from a row behind them walked up to the podium that had been set alongside the open grave: Charlotte Mayer and her son John.

"Good morning, everyone," she said, looking around the group, "John and I have made a decision, and in honor of Pete Ferris we would like to share that decision with you this morning." She put an arm around her son's shoulders and pulled him close as she spoke.

"This has been a difficult time. I don't have to tell you that. My son lost his father. Bridget lost her father. And Lewellyn lost the brother she dearly loved. As some of you know, Melanie, Pete's late wife, was my closest friend, and Pete, too, was a dear, dear friend of mine. Once in a while good things happen in strange ways. This is one of those times . . ." Her voice broke, and Lew could see she was struggling. "John and I learned two days ago that as Stanley Mayer's son he is heir to the McDonough estate. This is official. With that fact having been established, John and I have decided to donate the land along the Pelican River to the Nature Conservancy, to be protected in perpetuity from any commercial development." Charlotte paused to make eye contact with everyone sitting in front of her. "That means no mining. Ever."

The crowd was quiet for a brief moment before the applause broke out. Charlotte wiped tears from her cheeks as people rose to their feet. Twelve-year-old John beamed as his mother hugged him.

* * *

It wasn't until after the luncheon following the ceremony that Lew got back to her office. Erin was waiting for her.

"Hi, Chief, sorry to interrupt, but I need your approval on a new slogan for our campaign."

"Aren't we in good shape with our brochures and the television interviews you've had me do?" asked Lew.

"Nope. We have to tackle that twelve-point buck baloney," said Erin, referring to the ads running for Lew's opponent—photos of the twenty-something sheriff's deputy standing beside his trophy deer as if that qualified him to run a countywide law enforcement operation.

"I agree," said Lew with a grin. "It's not as though bucks and does and fawns are the bad actors challenging the McBride County Sheriff's Department."

"Right!" With that Erin whipped out a bumper sticker that she had been hiding behind her. The banner had a white background outlined in red; the words on it were printed in bright-blue with the exception of the word *for*, which was highlighted in brilliant red.

Erin held her breath and waited as Lew read: "Lew Ferris for Sheriff: The Woman Who Helped Save the Pelican River."

"But I didn't do that all alone," said Lew raising her eyes and protesting. "Think of all the people who helped me: Bruce Peters, Ray, Dani Wright, your father, Dr. Carter . . ."

"People know that, and they also know those are the people who will be working with you if you win. But this slogan works so well. It goes to the heart of why we need someone like you, Chief. Forget that hunk of venison hanging from a tree. We need someone who can keep our homes, our properties, our lakes and rivers and forests safe. Someone who knows how to save human lives—"

"All right, all right," said Lew. "'A hunk of venison?' Where did you get that phrase?" She had to laugh.

"Thought it up myself. Just now. Spur of the moment." Erin checked her watch. "Oops, gotta leave. Next meeting tomorrow, okay? We'll strategize where we are in the campaign then. I'll give you a call to set a time."

"Tomorrow is Saturday, I'm off."

"Not while you're running for office you're not." With a wave of her hand, Lew's campaign manager was gone.

Erin had just walked out the door when Lew's desk phone rang. It was Marlaine on Dispatch saying she had a visitor.

"Name?" asked Lew. "See if they can make an appointment for later." She looked at the stack of reports that had to get done that day.

"I've no idea who this is, Chief." Lew heard the smile in Marlaine's voice as she said, "I don't think they can wait. They're heading your way."

*Must be Doc*, thought Lew. He was the only person who could breach Marlaine's security.

But the door opened to a surprise. Not one visitor. Thirty: thirty seventh-graders from both classes at Curran School, thirty classmates of Mason and John, stood there with Erin's head visible right behind them.

"Where are your brochures, Chief Ferris?" asked John and Mason in concert. The kids stretched out their hands to Lew as Mason said, "We're going door-to-door for you all day tomorrow."

# Chapter Thirty-Four

∼

After spending her Saturday morning knocking on doors in the neighborhood Erin had assigned her, Lew needed a break. She really did not like running for office. Shaking hands, smiling, talking too much about herself—she hated it. Before noon she had made up her mind: *I will never run for president. That I promise.*

Before she could escape back to her office and the never-shrinking pile of reports tied to the three investigations, there was one more task that she needed to handle: deciding on a headstone for her family's plot.

During the ceremony at the gravesite she had noticed that merely a series of simple, flat gravestones marked where each of her family members was buried. Given that their numbers were increasing and at age fifty-three she could plan on joining them one of these years, she had decided to order a headstone for the Ferris family. But first, as up to now she hadn't spent much time thinking about headstones, she thought it wise to check out what other people did.

Driving down the narrow lane toward the area where her family was buried, she pulled up. Something was different. In front of the flat gravestones was an oblong gray-granite headstone. It had to be four feet high. She must be in the wrong place.

She walked around the large object and stopped, confused. Someone had put a headstone right where she was planning to have one installed herself. And it was engraved with a name she knew well: FERRIS.

The names of Peter, Melanie, her son Chris, and her parents were engraved on the headstone too. Though more than enough space remained for more names to be added, she couldn't believe what else she saw embedded in the granite below her family's name.

A simple but striking oval-shaped ceramic plaque was set into the granite stone and featured a loon floating on an azure background of water and sky. The bird had been captured in all its summer magnificence: the black head and dagger-like beak, the black-and-white striped collar encircling the slender neck, the snow-white breast, and the black-and-white checkerboard sloping across the bird's back.

Lew ran to the cemetery office. The door was unlocked, but the director was nowhere to be seen. As she was about to leave, one of the custodians walked in. She recognized

Duane Fries, a friend of Ray's. She knew that when money was tight Ray worked part-time at the cemetery.

"Duane, can you check and see who paid for that headstone on my family's plot?" she asked.

"Sure, we keep that information in a file right here," he said, pulling open a drawer in the tall metal cabinet behind the funeral director's desk.

He paged through it for a couple of minutes, then pulled up a sheet and looked at it. "No name, Chief Ferris, all it says here is 'gravedigger.' Sorry. Can't tell you more. Maybe the director knows. He'll be in tomorrow."

Lew got back in her cruiser. Then it dawned on her. Who had "gravedigger" emblazoned on the bug-catcher attached to the grill on his ancient pickup, the pickup with the floorboards missing under the driver's seat?

*How on earth?* Ray had so little money that he must have promised the artist and the owner of the headstone business a decade of guiding or a million bluegills, or maybe Netflix had coughed up a few grand for his documentary. She knew the latter wasn't likely.

Lew drove straight to the trailer home hidden behind the neon-green musky. She hoped he was home. She had to give the gravedigger a long, warm hug. She might have to cry a little too.

\* \* \*

Hours later as she lay beside Doc, his bedroom windows open to the lake breezes, she heard the eerie tremolo of a loon haunting the night air.

And she knew then that Pete was at peace.

# Acknowledgments

A warm thank-you to everyone who has helped make *Wolf Hollow* read well and look good. This includes Ben LeRoy, my good friend and editor, who got the ball rolling; Sara Henry with her excellent editing; and Nicole Lecht, who designed the stunning cover. But none of this could have happened without meticulous guidance from Melissa Rechter, assistance from Madeline Rathle, and the efforts of everyone on the Crooked Lane team—production and marketing—who have helped make *Wolf Hollow* possible.

You make me look good. Thank you!